Becoming *Pablo*

Teresa van Bryce

Handwritten Press

Copyright © 2021 by Teresa van Bryce
All rights reserved.
www.teresavanbryce.com

This book or any portion thereof may not be reproduced or used in any manner whatsoever without the express written permission of the publisher except for the use of brief quotations in a book review.

First edition, 2021
ISBN 978-1-9990872-0-3

Handwritten Press
Alberta, Canada

Publisher's Note: This is a work of fiction. Names, characters, and incidents are the products of the author's imagination and any resemblance to actual persons, living or dead is entirely coincidental. Locales and public names are sometimes used for atmospheric purposes.

For Nollind,
who's never afraid to reinvent himself,
and stands calmly by while I attempt to do the same.
The adventure continues...

Also by Teresa van Bryce:

House of the Blue Sea

The Double R
Cottonwood Wind

Acknowledgments

Although writing is a somewhat solitary venture, books are not written in isolation of others. I am deeply grateful to the following for their contributions to *Becoming Pablo*:

My beta readers, who took time out of their busy lives to read Pablo's story and offer their insights, suggestions, and observations: Nora Bitner, Susan Bitner, Gord Cochrane, Laurana Rayne, Barb Reimer, Nollind van Bryce, and Alex White.

My four-legged family—Chico, Nevada, Storm, Rosa, Hank, and Fran—who inspire me and keep me in the real world every day. (And I apologize to the horses and cats that none of your species were mentioned in the telling of this tale. Your turns are coming.)

My partner, friend, husband, and sounding board, Nollind, for driving the car while the idea for Pablo's story was born. Without you, there would have surely been a wreck.

One

The crunch of tires on gravel came as a surprise. Paul wasn't expecting anyone. All the reserved guests were checked in for the night and drop-ins were uncommon at Casa del Mar Azul.

He left the front desk, crossing the red tiles of the lobby to its arched entrance. The bougainvillea hung long and fragrant at the roof line, its bright pink flowers in full bloom.

A gray SUV sat parked in the loading area, a woman in the driver's seat. Her head rested on the steering wheel, blonde hair shining and wild in the late-day sunlight. She wasn't one of his guests and not anybody he recognized as a regular at the restaurant. No front plate adorned the vehicle to provide a clue.

Paul considered walking over and tapping on the window but, on an instinct, waited for the woman to exit the car on her own. As if sensing his presence, she lifted her head, staring a moment before swinging the door open and climbing out, hoisting a leather bag over one shoulder. Dressed in shades of blue, she wore a tunic top over a pair of faded jeans.

"Hello," Paul said from where he stood on the pebbled walkway. "Can I help you?"

"Hi." She hurried forward, rummaging in her purse. "Have I found the right place? Is this you?" A crumpled brochure was in her right hand and she stretched it toward him as she approached.

Paul recognized his brochure immediately, a piece he'd had printed when he first purchased and renamed the hotel. *Visit*

Casa del Mar Azul and drink in serenity scrolled across the front flap. "It is. I'm the owner."

The woman stopped, studying him. "You're British." It was a statement more than a question.

"Indeed, I am."

"Sorry … I didn't expect that. From the pamphlet I thought … well, it doesn't really matter." She glanced back toward the car. "I have a dog. I should have called to ask if you take pets. I'd been on the road for days when I saw the brochure and I just … well … he's small, my dog, Rufus, and very well behaved. If you don't take pets or have any rooms available, maybe you can point me someplace else. It's just that your brochure … well … this probably sounds ridiculous but … it … spoke to me."

Something about this woman didn't line up. She appeared to be in her late forties, but was like a teenager explaining why she'd been out past curfew. Her wavy hair rebelled in the humidity, and her face exhibited the strain of many hours on the road— not the look of a typical holidayer arriving at his Baja boutique hotel. But, whatever her story, before him stood a woman who needed his help. Paul offered a hand. "I'm Paul Hutchings. You and Rufus are quite welcome at Mar Azul."

She hesitated but then accepted his outstretched hand, gripping it as one might a lifeline. Her face stiffened and pools developed in her lower lids. "Thank you," she managed to say.

Before the tears could spill over, she turned away, moving to the passenger door and pulling it open. A small brown-and-white dog jumped down, his whiskered nose immediately on the ground discovering the scents of Mexico. When he spotted Paul he trotted over, tail wagging, and plopped his butt on the ground at Paul's feet.

"Well, hello, wee doggo." Paul knelt and rubbed the little dog's head and body. He didn't ordinarily have pets in the hotel, but he wasn't about to reveal his policy to this fragile-looking woman. He'd make it work. There was a modest room on the side with a separate entrance that would keep Rufus from any offended guests.

Blue canvas trainers made their way from the car, crunching across the pebbles. Paul stood. "I have just the room for you and your dog. It's small but allows easy access to the outdoors for any needed … business."

"Small is fine. Anything is fine. He's very quiet, and a terrier-cross so he doesn't shed much, and he's friendly to everyone, dogs, people, even cats."

"It's okay. Truly. The dog is okay."

She nodded and attempted a smile, but it vanished before it could form. "Okay. Good. Thank you. I'm Sandra."

"Let's get you checked in then, Sandra. I'll collect your bags when that's done." He passed through the archway, a flower-laden vine brushing the top of his head.

"I don't have a lot. I can get them myself."

Paul glanced over his shoulder. "It's not a problem at all. I have some time before—"

"I'd prefer to do it myself. Please."

He stepped behind the desk. "All right. There's a parking spot near the door to your room. You can drive down before you unload."

An audible breath escaped her. Did this woman have something in her car she didn't want seen? Was she running from someone? She had the manner of a person being chased. Whether by an actual or imagined threat was difficult to say.

Paul pulled a guest card from the drawer and picked up a pen. "So, Sandra …?"

"Lyall." She spelled her surname for him.

"And … American?"

"Canadian. From Alberta."

"Ah, you've come seeking warmth then. I visited your fair province about ten years ago. It's a lovely place, in autumn." There was no response to his familiarity with her homeland. "And the number plate on your car? It's a rental?"

"No, it's mine. The plate is Alberta … and … the …" She looked down at her feet and thumped her fist on the desk. "Damn it. I can't think of the license number."

Reaching across the counter, Paul placed a hand on hers to quiet it, a line he rarely crossed with his guests. "It's okay. I know which one is yours."

She nodded quickly and took a breath.

Paul requested a credit card and a piece of photo identification. The second piece of ID was not a normal ask, but he wanted to know this woman was who she claimed to be. He studied the photograph on her Alberta driver's license. Seemed she was legit.

"So you drove from Alberta to the near bottom of the Baja Peninsula. Impressive. That must have taken at least—"

"Four days."

"Blimey. I would have guessed five or six."

"I didn't stop a lot."

Driving four days straight to reach a hotel she hadn't known existed until discovering an old brochure which was unlikely to have circulated beyond Baja. "So, you found my brochure where? It's good to know, for marketing."

"In a place north of here where I stayed last night … something Villa maybe … or … sorry … I don't recall the name, or the town. I can look it up." She started digging in her bag.

"Not important," he said. "Just curious. I've not used these brochures in about four years." He placed a key on the desk. "So, you're all checked in. Are you hungry? I recently opened a restaurant on the beach side, Pablo's I call it, and dinner service begins in half an hour." Which reminded him he needed to get to the kitchen. Carmelita was exceedingly good at the prep but didn't like to cook the dinner menu.

"I've got snacks in the car. I'll be fine. Thanks."

Snacks? This woman had driven twenty-five hundred miles in four days and was planning to eat road snacks for dinner? Not on his watch. "Tell you what. I'm trying a new dish as a special tonight. Do you like fish?"

She nodded.

"I'm always looking for feedback on new recipes and could send a plate to your room, on the house. You can let me know tomorrow what you think of it, if I should put it on the menu. I'd appreciate your input."

"I … could do that. Fish would be … very nice."

Again the deep and audible breath. She was trying not to cry at every turn. This woman wasn't chased. She was in pain. Something Paul could relate to.

Two

7 Years Earlier — London, England

He'd spent an entire day getting home to London from the wilds of Northumberland and the train had been late and chock-a-block. Paul trudged the last block to the two-storey flat—a *maisonette* according to the estate agent—he shared with his wife.

He'd been fired, from a role for which he'd auditioned and earned fair and square. But the director had pulled in a family member to take the part. Sure, they'd paid a penalty, but what did that matter. It was the best role Paul'd had in five years—a launching pad, he'd thought. A friend had gone out on a limb for him, got him the audition, and he'd won over the casting director. All for naught.

At least he could look forward to surprising Rachel. She'd seemed distant and sad when she'd dropped him at the station a few days earlier, like she didn't want him to go. It was too late to cook her dinner, she'd likely grabbed takeaway on her way from the office, but it was a fine March evening and they could wander down to the pub for a drink. A pint might make the telling of his sad tale a little easier.

Paul wasn't the primary breadwinner in the relationship, but Rachel would nonetheless be disappointed. Her lawyer's salary at Forth and Hanson had been supporting them since they'd married six years earlier, and Paul worried she sometimes tired of carrying most of their financial commitments.

The main floor lights were on in their flat. Paul smiled. His wife was home.

He stopped to inhale the faint aroma of the cherry tree just starting to bloom. Rachel said the scent reminded her of roses, Paul claimed lilac, but they agreed on its sweet accent of vanilla. A flower-laden branch brushed his shoulder as he climbed the few stairs to the front door. It was time for a pruning.

Paul rummaged for keys in his small backpack. Three days of no use had relegated them to some deep corner of the bag beneath the latest issue of Fourthwall magazine, his ear buds, two Grisham novels, his faded Queens Park Rangers cap, and something wrapped in plastic he couldn't identify at a glance.

He pushed open the door, half expecting a startled Rachel to look up from her favourite chair in the front room, reading glasses perched on her nose. But the room was empty. With his wheeled suitcase parked by the umbrella stand, he kicked off his white trainers and went in search of his bride.

Two wineglasses sat on the kitchen counter, one a quarter full, the other empty. His head tipped toward his shoulder as he struggled to work things out in his mind. Maybe Gillian had come by for wine and they'd headed out from here? But it would be unusual for Rachel to leave lights on when going out for the evening.

There was a thump overhead and the sound of Rachel's laugh, an intoxicating sound that had reeled him in the first time they'd met. She loved old movies, especially comedies, and he envisioned her snuggled into bed with her iPad, watching Monty Python or Caddyshack for the umpteenth time, a box of gingersnaps and a cup of tea on the night table. Her predictability was one of the many things Paul loved most about his wife. The lengthy list also included that toned body he couldn't wait to get his hands on. She'd started going to a gym six months before, and the results were turning heads wherever they went. Although not a fitness fanatic, Paul couldn't deny that his already gorgeous wife had developed a glow from the additional exercise. He was nearly tempted to join her in her new fitness kick, feeling some pressure to keep up.

Two at a time, Paul bounded up the stairs.

The door to their bedroom was partway open and light shone in from the stairwell. He pushed the door wide, throwing light onto the queen-size bed and its jumble of blankets and limbs. Rachel's auburn hair lay sprayed across a white pillowcase. But he couldn't see her face beyond the man blocking his view, the man who was right this moment shagging his wife.

He stood, frozen in place. His wife and her lover didn't realize he was standing there, watching them have sex, in his bed, in his home. His wife.

Paul's heart thudded in his chest as his mind searched frantically for an explanation for the scene before him. Something other than his wife had a lover, that there was another man in his bed, that the love of his life was betraying him.

"Rachel. What in hell…?"

The dark-haired man rolled off to the side and he and Rachel stared wide-eyed at Paul from the bed.

"Paul? What are you doing here?"

"What am *I* doing here? Are you kidding me? I live here. Your husband. Remember? Or, it seems, no." His attention went to the frightened-looking guy with the perfectly-mussed coiffe. "And who the fuck is this?" He pointed. "Never mind. I don't care who you are. Get out of my bed. Get out of my house."

The man scrambled out from under the sheet and started gathering scattered clothing from the floor.

"Actually, you know what. Scratch that. I'll go. I'm clearly the one who doesn't belong here."

"Paul." Rachel wrapped herself in the bedsheet, like that would make a difference now, and jumped from the bed. "Wait."

"For what? For you to tell me how long this has been going on? Or how many there have been before this guy?" Paul whirled and stormed down the stairs, calling back over his shoulder, "Fuck you, Rachel!"

Grabbing his suitcase from the foyer, he slammed the door behind him hard enough, he hoped, to be felt upstairs. How could she do this to him? They'd been together for a dozen years, he'd waited bloody tables to support her through law school, and he'd trusted her completely. All the out-of-town jobs, it never crossed his mind to worry about what was happening at home. They were best friends, soul mates, and had what he thought was a healthy sex life. Where had things gone wrong? When?

When Paul reached the street, he stopped short. He had no clue what to do next, how to deal with this, where to go. The pub seemed a good start, but what self-respecting Englishman shows up at a pub with tears streaming down his face. Paul returned to the concrete stairs leading to his flat and collapsed onto the bottom step, head falling into his hands. "Bloody hell." He was most certainly not fit for a public place.

It was too late to head to his mum's in Cornwall and he couldn't face his younger sister and her perfect life in Highgate. His head fell back and he gazed up at the dark, gray sky. A single star reached out through the city's smog and light pollution. It was faint but visible.

Paul pulled his cell phone from a pocket, scrolled through his contacts, and touched *Mark Jeffery* on the list. "You're probably out of town and your wife would as soon spit on as talk to me, but you're my only hope, mate." He touched the green icon.

"Hello."

"Mark, hey, it's Paul." He did his best to keep his voice normal, whatever normal sounded like.

"I gathered it was you when your face appeared on my screen. What can I say? The modern world." Mark liked to tease.

"Of course. I didn't … think."

"Is everything all right? You sound a trifle wretched."

Where to begin? How much to tell? "Are you in London at the moment?"

"Happens I am."

"At home?"

"Paul. What's happened? Are you in trouble? Do you need me to come?"

Paul struggled to speak, his voice deserting him, the word *please* coming out like a croak.

"Where are you? What's the address? I'll be there as soon as I can." The sound of rustling fabric and the jingle of keys travelled through the phone line.

"My address. Our flat. I'm here in front."

The background noise ceased. "Well, that's a relief."

"Not sure I see it that way."

"Just taking the glass half full approach. You're not in hospital … or the nick."

"Now, why the hell would I be in jail, Jeffery?" Mark always managed to produce a smile, even in the worst of circumstances.

"You're certain you don't want to stop for a pint?" Mark asked. "You absolutely look like you could use a pint."

"I could, but I don't feel fit to be out in public tonight. Haven't you got a well-stocked bar in your mansion?"

"Of course, but Serena is home and, well, you know how she can be with—"

"With me? Like, not seeming to notice I'm in the room? Either that or she doesn't deem me worth speaking to."

"Right. Yes. Well, it's just that she's leaving to go on location in America tomorrow and can be even more … Serena … when preparing for a role."

"Actors," said Paul.

"Precisely."

Mark was also an actor, the most successful of them. He and Paul had attended acting school together twenty years earlier but, as swiftly as Mark's star had risen, Paul's plummeted, to the point where it had become a challenge to snag even a bit part in a low-budget television program. Mark had attained considerable fame playing Rochester in a BBC production of Charlotte Bronte's Jane Eyre, and lately was receiving calls from Hollywood producers. His days of auditioning were over. Maybe Paul's were as well.

"Okay, fine, a pub, but somewhere dark and empty."

"I know just the place." Mark signalled and turned left toward Central London.

"Christ, Hutchings, that is some dreadful homecoming. Cheating harlot. You've left her then?" Mark drank from his pint of pale lager.

"I suppose so. I—"

"Suppose so? You can't go back there now. You'd never be able to trust her again. Every time you leave to go on location you'll be wondering."

"I'm not convinced I'll be going on location anytime soon."

"What? Wait a minute. Shouldn't you be in Northumberland?"

Paul peered down into his beer glass. "Yes, I *should*, but I'm not. I was sacked and replaced before even getting on camera."

"But you aced the audition. The casting director rang to tell me so. She loved you."

"She may have, but not as much as the director loved his wife's cousin's brother, or whoever he was. They paid me out and sent me packing."

"Well, isn't that a load of bollocks. I'm sorry, mate. I had no idea."

"And then I went home to find my wife in bed with some younger-than-me bloke with a full head of splendid hair." Paul ran his hand through his thinning blond hair, his forehead much taller than it once was.

"I'm sure hair has nothing to do with anything."

Says the guy with more hair than most twenty-year-olds. Paul didn't envy his friend many things, but his full head of wavy, brown hair was one of the few. It always looked a little unkempt and yet somehow perfect. "Maybe not, but it's easier to blame my lack of hair than my capacity as a husband."

"Well, you can stay with us for now. Serena will be gone for at least a few weeks so you won't have to worry about those icy stares. I've grown accustomed to them but, in your condition, I think you have need of a more tender touch."

Paul snorted. "And you'll provide this 'tender touch'?"

"Of course. Haven't we always been there for each other? In sickness and in health?"

It was true. They had.

Three

Seated on the hotel's rooftop patio, Paul watched the sun as it rose from the Sea of Cortez. The light reflected golden on the rolling waves, their rhythmic whoosh and thump like a sound-track for his life. Just another day in paradise. In ten years, he'd never tired of this scene.

The beach was empty at this hour of the morning, no sign yet of his Canadian guest. In the three days since her arrival, he'd hardly caught sight of her. She'd ordered a few breakfast items for her bar fridge and taken all other meals in her room. From the kitchen window, he'd spotted her walking on the beach every morning, always a good distance from the hotel, cutting a path along the water's edge, Rufus scampering just ahead of her.

Although it was Paul's nature to help, Sandra appeared to need her space. She'd booked in for another week, so there was still time to reach out, when the time was right. There would be live music in Pablo's tonight, a new musician in the area from Canada via Cabo San Lucas. A fellow Canadian on the stage seemed a good excuse to lure Sandra Lyall from the solitude of her room.

Paul lifted himself out of the white Adirondack chair, taking one last look at the sun, now above the horizon, cutting a golden path across the waves to Casa del Mar Azul. This place was a haven for him and he understood more than anyone its powers to heal. Where would he have ended up if not for his house of the blue sea?

———

"Ms. Lyall!" Paul called to her as she turned up the path to the hotel after her morning walk. He'd been keeping an eye from the kitchen window.

She waved and Rufus ran to Paul's feet as fast as his short legs could manage.

"Please, call me Sandra." She was breathless from her barefoot walk in the deep sand.

"It's a lovely morning. Pleasant walk?"

The fresh air and exercise had added a flush to Sandra's cheeks and, despite her windblown hair, she was looking more put together than when she'd arrived.

"We did. Rufus loves the beach. We're landlocked in Alberta, so the ocean is a novel experience for him."

"And everything is okay with your room, with your stay?"

"It's great, thanks." Her eyes darted toward the hotel. "Well, I should put something in my stomach."

"Breakfast is being served on the south patio until eleven if you'd like something more substantial than granola. I've got an omelette special this morning, ham and mushroom. Guests rave about my omelettes." She was starting to fidget. "Or, if not breakfast, maybe you'd like to come to Pablo's for dinner later. There's live music tonight, a singer-songwriter from Canada."

The furtive look dissipated. "Oh …"

"The lounge opens at five, dinner service starts at six, and the music begins at seven."

"That actually sounds … nice. I might do that." Sandra started to leave and then angled back toward him. "Pablo's … is it named for you? It's Spanish for Paul, isn't it?"

It was the first time she'd shown interest in anything beyond surviving the moment.

"It is. The previous owner called me Pablo, as do the locals on occasion. It seemed a natural fit."

"I'll try to come, see how I feel later."

"My staff and I will do everything we can to make you comfortable."

She nodded, but her eyes suggested it wouldn't happen.

"There's a bar if you'd rather not sit alone at a table and—"

"I'll think about it. Thanks."

She continued along the path, giving a quick whistle to Rufus.

Had he pushed too hard? The line between ignoring and overwhelming was difficult to tread.

Situated on the ground floor of Casa del Mar Azul, Pablo's faced the beach and the Sea of Cortez. When Paul first acquired the hotel, the guests travelled to San Leandro for everything but his continental breakfast and, although the village was just a ten-minute drive via winding road or a half-hour walk along the beach, he wanted to offer a more complete get-away. With just fifteen rooms in the hotel, he couldn't launch an all-inclusive experience, but he could provide a full breakfast and an evening drinking and dining spot.

Although small, San Leandro had a reasonably large area population, many of them ex-pats from America and Canada. Pablo's clientele grew as word got out that a new restaurant was open for business. Keeping the menu small and focusing on daily specials made it work, often featuring the day's catch from local fishermen.

Live music had been a natural fit with a varied collection of artists in the area. Paul tried to offer entertainment two or three nights a week, paying the performers with food and drink and encouraging tips.

Tonight's entertainment was a new arrival to San Leandro, a Canadian who'd been living in Cabo San Lucas for a few years. He'd stopped by with a recorded demo a few weeks back and

Paul was delighted to book him for the first open date in the calendar.

Paul unhooked and coiled the rope barrier that hung across the entrance to the restaurant. Pablo's had been a stone patio when he purchased the hotel and he'd retained its outdoor feel, keeping it fully open on the sea side. The waterfront tables always filled first.

Carmelita was at work in the kitchen, cutting up tomatoes for the evening special, and she looked up when he entered. "*Buenas tardes, Señor* Paul." Her round face glistened in the warm kitchen.

"Buenas tardes. Is Elena here yet?"

Elena was Carmelita's seventeen-year-old daughter who Paul had hired when Pablo's opened. Although inexperienced, she was a lovely girl and good with the customers in her quiet way.

"She had sports after school. She will be here very soon."

Carmelita lived nearby with her two children, and Paul hired her when he bought the hotel. The previous owner had family to assist with running the place, but Paul was only Paul and, even though Mar Azul was a small place, he'd needed the help. Once the restaurant opened, he'd expanded Carmelita's hours and duties to include breakfast and dinner prep and a bit of cooking. She was a marvel with basic Mexican fare and Paul often drew on her ideas and experience. His recipes were frequently a combination of traditional Mexican and international favourites.

As he dropped garlic and tomatoes into a pan to start the evening special, he thought of Sandra Lyall. He hoped she'd venture down for dinner. It was difficult to be supportive when she seldom left her room, but he had to admit she'd looked brighter today, even without his interference.

Elena burst through the back door, her younger brother in tow. "Buenas tardes. I am sorry to be late."

"Arturo, you are supposed to be at home tending the chickens," Carmelita said.

"I am finished, Mama. Elena said I can help with the tables." The young man looked at Paul. "For no charge. Elena has offered me part of her tips for my help."

The work ethic of the Flores family continually astounded Paul. His experience of young people in the UK was mostly cell phones and hanging out. "Help is always appreciated. Maybe we can talk about some other jobs that need doing, for actual wages. How old are you now, Arturo?"

The boy's face lit up in a bright smile. He was a good-looking kid, and always polite. The guests would like him.

"I am sixteen."

Carmelita continued with her work, not looking up. "You are fifteen."

"But only until the summer. I'm old enough to have a job. Elena is just seventeen."

Arturo and Elena's father was killed in a fishing accident when they were small children, and Carmelita had worked multiple jobs to support the family ever since. Paul was always happy to contribute to the Flores household.

"When would you like that I start, Mister Paul?" Arturo asked.

"Well, if it's okay with your mother, tomorrow after school. How's that?"

Arturo nodded his head with enthusiasm, but glanced sideways at Carmelita.

She wiped her hands on her apron and approached the two of them, taking Arturo's face between her hands. "If you promise that your school comes first then, yes."

"I promise." Arturo wrapped his arms around his mother, and she smiled at Paul over the boy's shoulder. She was no more than five feet tall and her son had bested her height in the past year.

Elena held a tray loaded with napkins and cutlery. "Come, little brother. We have work to do."

When they were beyond earshot, Paul said, "And *I* promise, too, that his school work will come first."

Carmelita took one of Paul's hands between hers. "You are a godsend, Pablo. You have helped my family so much."

"And you've helped me even more. I couldn't run this place without you, and now your children. It's a win-win."

"Win-win? What is this?"

Although she spoke English very well, Carmelita was frequently stumped by expressions or slang.

"It's like you win and I win. We both benefit from the arrangement."

"Ah. Si. Win-win. Si."

Since he spent most of his evenings cooking in back, Paul gave a description of Sandra to Elena and Arturo. He was at the grill when Arturo hurried into the kitchen. "I think the lady is here, Mister Paul." Carmelita's children were taught to respect their elders, and he couldn't convince them to call him Paul without prefacing it with señor or mister.

"Ah, brilliant. Carmelita, can you keep an eye on this for me?"

Paul stepped from the kitchen to the restaurant, warmed by the familiar scene. The sound of the waves, the low light from the lanterns, and the clink and murmur of happy diners.

Sandra Lyall stood at the entrance glancing around the restaurant, looking like she might bolt if not settled in a hurry. She wore a full-length, pale-blue denim skirt with the same tunic top she'd arrived in and, oddly, the same canvas sneakers.

"Ms. Lyall. Welcome to Pablo's." He hustled over to her. "So glad you've joined us."

"Thanks … I didn't have much to wear for dinner attire and," she glanced down at her feet, "and just the one pair of warm-weather shoes."

"You're fine. This is Mexico and we're almost on the beach. Casual attire is altogether appropriate." He placed a hand behind her shoulder. "Come in. Come in. Would you like to sit at the bar or would you prefer—"

"Where will the music be?"

"Over in the front corner there. You can gaze at the sea and the musician at the same time."

Sandra's eyes scanned the restaurant before landing on the area Paul indicated. She pointed to a bright-blue bar stool closest to the stage. "I guess I'll take that one then."

"Excellent choice. I'll send Elena over with a menu. The special tonight is a traditional Mexican dish with a Pablo's twist, Yellowfin tuna and avocado enchiladas."

"That'll be fine. No need for a menu."

With Sandra seated he said, "I'm pleased to see you here."

The bar itself was Paul's creation, a simple plywood structure covered in white plaster and topped with a thick slab of red-brown wood. Sandra ran a hand over the smooth surface. "What beautiful wood."

"It's Parota, a gift from a woodworker friend who lives in La Paz. I'm afraid it rather outclasses the plain, white base I built."

Sandra leaned back to view the plastered front of the bar. "Maybe it just needs a little of the beach, some shells or coral, that kind of thing."

"What a terrific idea. You have a designer's eye. If you find anything appropriate on your beach walks, I'd welcome the contribution."

"And I'd welcome a reason to collect some of the beautiful things I run across each day. I was going to squirrel a few away for the trip home, but it's probably best to leave the treasures here where they belong."

"I have to get back to the kitchen, but you'll let me know if you need anything tonight? Anything at all."

"I was going to request a glass of water but, you know, I think I'd like one of those special Pablo's-sized margaritas on your chalkboard." She gestured to the handwritten sign behind the bar.

"Of course. Blended or on the rocks, and salt or no?"

"On the rocks with salt, please."

It was only a spark, but the light that turned on when she spoke of using beach treasures to enhance his bar, like a sliver of the real Sandra Lyall shone through the cracks of desperation, gave Paul hope that Cortez was performing another healing.

Everyone fed and contentedly sipping their wine or savoring a cup of coffee, Paul escaped the kitchen to mingle with his guests. It was his favourite time of day, when the work was done and he could savour the fruits of his labour. The restaurant was about half full, a typical evening when the hotel was less than fully booked.

The performer, Ian LeRoy, was a hit. He had an excellent repertoire, was happy to take requests, and had some very good originals. This guy was worth far more than a burger and a beer, but hopefully it would be enough to bring him back.

Paul and Ian were probably close in age, in their late forties, but Ian's red-blond hair worn shoulder length in back made him look younger. With double necklaces made of beads and leather and a diamond stud in one ear, he rather reminded Paul of Kenny Loggins.

Ian finished a Jimmy Buffet favourite, *Cheeseburger in Paradise*, and placed his guitar in the stand. "I'm going to take a short break. Drop your requests in the tip jar and I'll play them if I can remember them."

He left the stage and stepped over to where Paul stood behind the bar. "Señor Hutchings. Thanks for the gig. The audience isn't large, but they make up for it with their enthusiasm."

"Sounding great, even better than your demo. And, please, call me Paul."

"And nothing quite like the background sound of the sea to round out a performance. Beautiful spot." Ian cast a glance around the room. "Is this a normal crowd?"

"It varies. I'm only just starting to get clients beyond my hotel guests so when the rooms are full, so is the restaurant. We're expecting a full house this weekend … if you're still up for two more nights."

"Yes, absolutely. I've bought a house in San Leandro so I'm content to be a regular for you, if your calendar has openings."

"For your kind of talent, openings are something we have plenty of."

Ian gave a nod of his head. "Well, thanks. I appreciate that."

Sandra was only a few feet away on her bar stool, able to hear the entire conversation but not showing any sign that she was listening.

"You're Canadian, aren't you, Ian?" Paul asked.

"I am, from la belle province, Quebec."

His French accent was flawless. "Ah, so bilingual, then."

"Tri, if you count my butchered efforts at Spanish. Knowing French helps a little, but I often end up speaking something I like to call Sprench."

Paul caught the hint of a smile on Sandra's face as she sucked the last of her drink out of the bottom of the hand-blown margarita glass. She *was* paying attention.

"At least you have the background in wrapping your mouth around sounds other than English. I feel like I speak Spanish with a perfect British accent. It's not even worthy of being called Spanglish." He glanced over at Sandra. Her drink was empty and she pushed the glass away from her.

"Can I get you a drink, Ian? Beer, wine, margarita?"

"*Cerveza, por favor.* Dos Equis amber if you have it."

Paul pulled a bottle from a cooler below the bar and popped the cap off, sliding it across to Ian. "Enjoy." He turned to Sandra. "And, Ms. Lyall, can I mix you another margarita?"

"No, I don't think so. This one was delicious, but also very large. I should—" She began to slide from her stool.

"How about some coffee then, or maybe a nice cup of tea?"

She settled. "Tea. Hm. I don't suppose you have peppermint?"

"Only the finest organic variety on the market." He'd find the biggest teapot they had. This woman needed to stay in the company of others a little longer. On his way to the kitchen, he turned, offhandedly. "Oh, and Ian, Sandra here is a fellow Canadian."

When Paul returned with the pot of steeping tea, Ian was parked on the stool beside Sandra and had engaged her in conversation.

"So you've lived in Mexico how long?" she asked.

"Oh, three or six years, give or take a decade. Time flies when you're the life of the Cabo party."

Was that a smile? Not a big, change-your-face affair, but her mouth was undeniably turned up at the corners.

Paul placed the teapot and a cup on the bar in front of Sandra.

"Thank you," she said, the gratitude in her eyes much greater than those two small words.

Ian played another set, a full hour, and still Sandra stayed. She ordered more tea and continued to watch and listen, clapping after each number, brightening at each of Ian's jokes. The rest of the crowd had also stayed. Mr. Le Roy was a highly engaging entertainer. What good fortune to have him in the neighbourhood. This guy would draw people, maybe even from the city of La Paz forty-five minutes north.

Ian finished his show with Margaritaville, the last piece of paper in his tip jar. "Thanks, everyone. You've been a great audience. See you here tomorrow night at seven. Paul tells me he's cooking up something extra special for the evening meal."

Paul had said nothing of the sort, but he wouldn't complain about having his special promoted. Although reliable patrons, his guests had options outside of Pablo's. He'd need to come up with something interesting for a Saturday night meal.

Ian set his guitar in the stand and came back to the bar, hopping onto the stool next to Sandra. "Well, fellow Canuck. Passable?"

"You were great. Like an elixir after a long week."

"Sandra drove down here from Alberta," Paul said.

"What? No way! At this time of year? Did you need to break trail through the Rockies?" He mimed pushing his way through snow.

She let out a little sound, almost a laugh. "It was actually alright after Great Falls in northern Montana. I drove in blinding snow for the first part."

"So, you've not heard of Westjet?"

Again, the near chuckle. "I just felt like driving. It was kind of … an impromptu trip. I hopped in the car and, a few days later, ended up here." She looked at Paul then, her eyes shining. "Lucky me."

Ian was observing her, as though trying to read between the lines of her story. Before Paul could divert the conversation elsewhere, Ian asked, "So what act of God prompts a multi-day journey across two borders and lands you exactly," he tapped a finger on the bar, "here."

Sandra stared at the teacup in her hands.

Paul held his breath.

"Well, that's a tale for another time." Sandra slid off her stool. "I'm ready for bed. Goodnight, gentlemen."

The two men watched her leave, her long skirt swinging as she hurried from the restaurant.

"Something I said?" Ian asked.

"I'm afraid so, old chap." He slapped Ian on the shoulder.

"Do you know her story?"

"That's the most I've heard of it. She's kept to herself until tonight."

"Well, hopefully I didn't run that onto the rocks."

"Doubtful. She might just need some space. Sometimes we need to hide away and lick our wounds when they're fresh."

Four

London, England

The knocking grew louder and more insistent. Paul lifted his head from the pillow. "What?"

"Having you here is akin to having a teenager, Hutchings." It was Mark. "And there's an incredibly good reason I have no offspring. Get out here and join me for breakfast."

"Not hungry. Thanks."

The door swung open and Mark was in the room, raising the blind to allow mid-morning light to enter. "Have you been in here since I left?" Mark had been away for three days meeting with the producers of his next movie. "Certainly smells like it."

He sat down on the edge of the bed. "Okay, what happened? You were very nearly ready to rejoin humanity when I left."

Paul pulled the pillow out from under his head and dragged it over his face. "I don't want to talk about it."

Mark grabbed the pillow, tossing it to the floor. "But I do, and this is my house."

Paul groaned. "Is this that 'tough love' thing they speak of for alcoholics?" Propping himself on one elbow, he rubbed at his face with the other hand.

"Well, you look rather crap. Were you drinking last night?"

"No. I was talking. To my cheating, lying whore of a wife."

"Ah, that would do it. But good for you. Two weeks was long enough for radio silence. I thought if I left you alone for a bit you might venture down that dark road."

"And it was very dark indeed." Paul hoisted himself up, retrieved the pillow from the floor and stuffed it between his back and the headboard. "I'm not confident I can manage this, Mark. I'm not cut out for tragedy. Tragicomedy maybe, but there's nothing funny in this."

"I don't know about that. You looking a fright surrounded by days of dirty socks and crisp packets is amusing … in a tragic sort of way."

Paul tried to laugh, but there was only a short outward breath in its place.

"But, seriously, what did she say …" Mark placed a hand on Paul's forearm. "… your cheating, lying whore of a wife."

"I feel just a little better to hear someone else refer to her in those terms. Thank you."

"My pleasure. What are friends for if not to tear down the ones we love and hate? Such a fine line."

Paul stared up at the ceiling, its stippled pattern a vast, snowy wasteland of mountain ranges, and tried to keep the tears from coming again, as they had been so frequently for two weeks. He'd swung between fury and devastation with barely a breath in between. Although never one of those *I don't cry* kind of men, he'd reached a whole new plateau of expressing his emotions. More accurately, he'd become a complete bawl-baby.

"Mister full head of hair, that I found in bed with *my* wife, works at her law firm. He's another lawyer. *Jeremy*. Younger than me. Younger than her. It's been going on for months. Months. Can you believe that? The thought of making love to her after she was … with … someone else just makes my heart feel as if someone's reached in and ripped it from my chest." Paul took a deep breath, quelling the rush of adrenalin. "They're in love, she says. Which is amusing because I understood that's what we were. In love. Not to mention married, with vows of honouring and cherishing and all that rubbish."

Mark nodded. "Right. And so it's done then. No reconciling, no cries for forgiveness."

"Far from it. Without saying the actual words, the message was that I should be the one crying for forgiveness, for neglecting our marriage, neglecting her."

Mark snorted. "Was it the supporting her through law school or the gourmet meals after a long day at the firm she found so neglectful?"

"I think it came down to money and career. Over the past year she's dropped a few hints about me giving up on acting and getting a 'real job'. We'd always supported each others' passions, so I didn't believe she was serious, or that it could lead to this."

"I'm certain it's not the only thing that led to this. Some people are wired to cheat. Didn't she have a boyfriend when she met you? Do it for you, do it to you? She'll do the same thing to Barrister Hairy at some point." Mark patted Paul's blanket-covered leg and stood. "Okay, enough nurturing, time for more of that tough love. We're going out for breakfast and I expect you showered and ready in half an hour."

The air was heavy with moisture as they set out for what Mark claimed to be the finest breakfast on the west side. "Are you certain you wouldn't rather drive? It's at least half an hour," Mark said.

Paul hadn't even opened his umbrella, allowing the light rain to moisten his thinning hair. "I'm hoping a long walk in the rain will prepare me for reentry to society."

"I'm afraid we'll require more time for that endeavour, so perhaps we should take the long route. Although, I'm not sure the restaurant will admit you, looking like you just climbed out of the Thames."

Paul batted Mark with his unopened umbrella. "I prefer your nurturing side. Can we go back to that?"

"No, sorry mate, you've reached your quota this morning. Maybe I'll tuck you in with a mug of cocoa upon our return. You're likely to have caught your death by then and will need some time in bed." Mark grabbed Paul's umbrella from him, opened it and passed it back. "You're getting soaked."

"Fine." Paul raised the umbrella over his head. "Is Serena still expected back next week?"

Mark nodded. "Yes, I'm afraid so. She … well …"

"What?"

"We'll sort it later."

"I'd prefer to deal with it here on the street than in a crowded cafe."

"Right. Well, she said you need to be gone when she gets home. But it's not for her to say. The house is half mine, entirely mine if you consider who paid for it. You'll stay as long as you need. But—"

"I must endure the icy stares and wrath of Serena."

"Well, yes. But I can offer some tips there." Mark grinned at Paul from under his umbrella. "I'm an old hand."

"Is everything all right, in your marriage?"

"Has it ever been? But, no, not really. We're headed toward a split, I'm certain." Mark picked up the pace.

"Did something happen?"

"No. Nothing concrete. She's just Serena and I'm me and we never should have married. Every marriage of celebrities should pass through a validation process to establish there's something beneath the evening gowns and tuxedos." The pace increased again. "But let's stay with *your* broken marriage, shall we? One car crash at a time."

"And how about we slow down a little so I can breathe enough to speak," Paul managed to gasp.

Mark stopped in the middle of the pavement. "Sorry. The

topic of my wife gets me agitated, particularly now when I want to support a friend." Mark looked up into the red dome of his umbrella as if searching for something. "Problem is, this meeting I've just come from, with my producers. The filming will be in Australia. I'm leaving in a week. I can be a buffer as long as I'm home, but you don't want to be under the same roof as Serena when I'm not." He began walking.

Paul watched his feet making their way along the wet pavement, his white trainers glowing against the dark background. Where would he go? No home. No job. No wife. No life, really.

Mark put a hand on Paul's arm and pulled him around to a stop. "I want to help you. I do. But I can't do it from Australia. I'm sorry."

Paul's eyes returned to his two feet as they resumed their step-by-step journey along the pavement.

But maybe Mark could help from Australia. He might see it as comparable to having a pitiful little brother asking to tag along, but nothing ventured, nothing gained. "Unless I go with you."

Mark remained silent, his eyes not leaving the pavement. Had he not heard? And then his face turned toward Paul and broke into that screen idol smile of his, white teeth lined up perfectly in his symmetrical face. "Now that, my old friend, is a smashing idea."

Five

Sydney, Australia

Paul gazed out at the view from Mark's tenth floor hotel room as the sun rose over Sydney Harbour. Sun. So much sun. He'd always lived in England and not travelled outside the United Kingdom his entire life. Overcast seemed homey and familiar, but oh how the Australian sun helped to brighten his mood.

They'd been in Sydney for a week and the first four days were like a holiday, he and Mark taking in some local tourist attractions. They'd visited the Sydney Opera House, climbed the Harbour Bridge, and enjoyed lunch and too many local beers at Bondi Beach. For three glorious days Paul had nearly erased the image of full-head-of-hair Jeremy on top of his wife.

But now it had returned, in high-definition technicolour. With Mark away for a few days on location, time alone had sent Paul's thoughts spiraling into dark places. And there'd been nightmares, where he climbed the stairs of his flat to find Rachel in bed with not one, but three young lawyers from her firm.

Paul didn't do solitude well. He'd grown up with four siblings, two older and two younger, and was a very contented middle child. Old enough to keep pace with big brothers and young enough to play with kid sisters, he never wanted for company.

Once in school, his social network only expanded with his natural ability to make friends.

When they'd been boys and then young men, Mark hadn't been a loner either, but his companion was always a doting girlfriend with another two or three waiting on the sidelines in the event the current girl didn't work out. Mark was never at loose ends for female company.

Paul couldn't shake his *big brother* role with girls and then women. He'd lost count of the number of times he'd heard those dreaded words, *you're like a brother to me.* No teenage boy wants to be any teenage girl's *just like a brother.*

It all changed in his graduation year when he'd met Jenna, who didn't see him as a brother or buddy.

Paul picked at the cuticles on his right hand. He hadn't thought about Jenna in a long while.

She'd been a small-town girl from northern England until her father died and she and her sister and mother moved south to live with extended family. Sweet was the best description of Jenna, with the prettiest eyes he'd ever seen, like pools of green glass. They'd been inseparable through their final year of high school and into his first years at LAMDA, the London Academy for Music and Dramatic Art. Jenna was an artist and took a job in a framing shop, her mother unable to afford art school tuition. Determined to teach herself the craft, Jenna enrolled in evening classes. Between the demands of their busy lives and the geographical bulk of London between them, Paul and Jenna's time together dwindled to weekends.

He preferred to think they just drifted apart. But, truthfully, one evening after classes, out with a group of his mates, he met a friend's sister, Rachel Stapleton. She was smart, ambitious, beautiful, and, much to his surprise, set her sights on him.

Rachel became a regular member of the evening pub crowd with her brother and his friends and, the more interest she showed, the more often Paul made excuses to Jenna why he couldn't see her that weekend. He never cheated on her, in a physical sense, but Rachel was always in his thoughts. Before asking Rachel out the first time, he met with Jenna and broke it off. He made his choice and had been happy with it for many years.

But now, here he sat, decades later, paying the price for that choice. Paul hadn't learned of Rachel's engagement until after they'd been together a while. She was somebody's fiancé when they'd met and still engaged the first time Paul slept over at her place. It bothered him when he found out but, ultimately, she'd chosen him. Wasn't that enough?

Staring out at Sydney Harbour, Paul wondered where Jenna was now. They'd maintained no common friendships after high school, so he'd not heard word of her since the day he broke their relationship and her heart. She'd cried, sobbed more accurately, and when he'd tried to hold her, be that big brother he'd always dreaded being, she'd pushed him away and stormed out. It was the last time he saw her.

Paul flipped open his laptop. It was rare for someone to *not* be found on the Internet these days. Maybe Jenna had a web page or a profile on Facebook. He typed her name into the search bar and got a list of Jenna Howards along with a group of images. He scanned the faces, landing on a familiar smile. The link took him to the web page of Jenna Howard, artist. There was a list of showings of her work, many of them at London galleries, some in Brighton and Bristol, and she taught classes at her home studio in Brighton. She'd always loved the sea, they both had. She was living her dream, or so it appeared online.

He hesitated to click on the bio page. Did he want to know she was happily married with two children and a cocker spaniel?

He clicked.

Only one child, and the dog was a cat, but the happily married seemed a fit. He gazed at her photo. Beyond some faint lines around the eyes and mouth, she looked just the same. That captivating smile and those incredible eyes. She wore her brown hair much shorter than when they'd dated, when it hung long and luxurious around her face.

Jenna. The one who got away?

Paul closed the lid on her happily-married face. This rabbit hole would lead nowhere productive. He'd go for a walk, soak up some of that healing Aussie sunshine. Mark would be back in a few days and they'd visit more of the local sights. In the meantime, he could do this alone thing.

Paul sat at one end of the long table, nursing a second lager. Mark and his colleagues from the film were back in Sydney and invited Paul along on an evening out. It had sounded like an excellent idea, especially after a solo week of wandering Sydney's streets and haunting their pubs and coffee shops. It was as though he'd lost his make-friends-easily talent, or Rachel had broken it. Broken described the feeling precisely, like something inside had shattered when he climbed those stairs and it affected his every interaction with the human race.

Tonight was no different. It started off grand with introductions all around, everyone delighted to meet the best friend of their leading man. That's how Mark had introduced him, as his best friend. The affection had touched Paul, but, as the questions came his way, he retreated. *Are you an actor too? Which films are you in? Are you working on something in Australia?* At least they didn't ask about his marriage. Movie people were more interested in your resumé than your love life. But the career questions weren't any easier to answer. *Am I an actor? Sure, although I generally spend my days dreaming up new recipes to surprise my wife. Oh, there she is, the wife. The wife I found in bed with another guy while I was out-of-town getting fired from the first acting job I'd had in almost a year. Films, let's see. Well, if you count waiter number two in that low-budget comedy and newspaper stand guy in the Harvey*

Woodward thriller. And am I working on something? Why yes, as a matter of fact, not killing myself.

Paul swallowed the last of his beer before standing and navigating the crowded pub to Mark's chair. He got his attention and leaned in. "I'm heading out."

"What? No. Stay. This gang will be here until they shut the place, if our time in the outback was any indication."

"Just what I don't want. You stay. I'll see you back at the hotel later. I need some air." Before Mark could further his argument, Paul was out the door and walking in the opposite direction from the hotel. Alone in a crowd, alone in their room. Neither appealed.

"I'd like to get out of Sydney for a bit, find some quiet," Paul said.

Mark sat across the table, room service breakfast sprawling between them. "Can't go, mate. Sorry. We're shooting here and then a location in the Blue Mountains."

"I didn't expect so. I'll be fine on my own. I've booked the train north this afternoon. Feeling like some time seaside."

"Of course. Understandable." Mark was spreading Vegemite on a piece of toast but stopped and looked at Paul. "And I'm sorry about last night. People are annoyingly curious creatures."

"It's fine. But not an experience I care to repeat. And I don't want to keep you from your colleagues. I'm sure you'd rather spend free time with them than your old down-in-the-dumps mate."

"It's not that at all. It's simply a part of the process for me, connecting with people off set. Truth be told, I'd much rather go back to Bondi with you. In fact, I envy your freedom to explore up the coast. If you stay awhile, maybe I can join you next time I have a few-day break?"

"I'd like that. Unless I've hopped a sailboat to America by then."

"Is that something you're considering?" Mark's brows scrunched above his brown eyes.

"Anything is possible. There was an ad online, a boat looking for crew, and the thought wasn't objectionable. But I haven't sailed in a very long time, and this particular vessel needed experienced hands. And mine most certainly do not qualify." He lifted his hands above the table and showed his palms to Mark. "Perhaps I'll find a crew needing a cook."

"They'd be lucky to have you. But please don't leave on my account. The down-in-the-dumps version of you is still better company than everyone else."

"But then you've always been a bit of a curmudgeon when it comes to meeting new people."

"I wouldn't be if most of them weren't so dreadfully dull."

"Such a snob." Paul crumpled up his napkin and lobbed it at Mark.

Six

Nambucca Heads, NSW, Australia

Mark insisted on booking Paul a room at a Coffs Harbour resort. It was spectacular and for two days Paul indulged in the posh surroundings and seafood buffets. But, the longer he stayed, the more he noticed the other guests in the resort. Couples. Many of them actual or behaving like newlyweds. He started spending more time roaming the beach than lounging by the pool, and sought out quiet, local diners for his meals. When he'd stayed to the end of Mark's gifted week, it was time for something different.

The something different turned out to be a backpackers accommodation down the coast at Nambucca Heads. He was twice the age of his fellow holidayers, but at least he didn't feel like the lone duck flying alongside the vee of mated-for-life geese.

The modest hotel sat right on the beach and, in addition to its dorm-style rooms, had four tiny sleeping cabanas off to one side. Paul rented a cabana for less than a quarter of the nightly rate of the Coffs Harbour resort, paying up front for a week's stay. There was no wifi, but the coffee shop up the road had service, and he sent Mark an email to advise him he was still on the continent and would be away for at least another week.

Although communal, having a kitchen was a treat. Paul purchased fresh fish and vegetables from the local market and created meals to rival the best of his weeks of restaurant dining. And his untypical-for-backpacker fare drew a lot of attention from the other patrons and the owners.

"Smells amazing in here." Georgiana hung her head over a pan and waved the aroma to her nose with a hand. "De-lish. What time is tea, then?" She smiled at him, her crooked teeth somehow a perfect fit in her round face. Georgiana and her husband, Romero, were the proprietors of the Nambucca Backpacker Hotel.

"There's plenty. I don't know how to cook for one person so you and Romero are welcome to join me."

"I'm kidding. But it smells fantastic. Are you a chef?" Georgiana was a native of Australia and had a broad accent.

"No. I simply like to create with food. My wife is, was, a bit of a foodie, so we were a good fit." And just like that, thoughts of Rachel led to thoughts of her and Jeremy which led to mental images of—. "Please. Join me for dinner. I'd love the company."

"Okay then. We'll bring the plonk."

"Sorry?"

"The wine, mate. We'll bring the wine."

"Right. Great. My outdoor table in half an hour?"

Georgiana and Romero arrived with two bottles of Australian wine, one red and one white. "We weren't sure which colour you like, so we brought one of each." Georgiana placed both bottles in the middle of the table and Romero produced three Lexan glasses from a shoulder bag.

"Welcome to my humble table. Please. Sit." The table, an old, four-legged affair, was constructed of wood with two painted chairs, one yellow and one red. "Oh…"

Before Paul could say anything more, Romero was dashing back toward the main building.

"He'll fetch a third chair," said Georgiana.

Paul uncovered the pan containing the Barramundi with

lemon butter sauce and his guest immediately leaned in. "I grew up on a sheep farm in central Australia and haven't eaten lamb or mutton since. But I never tire of fish no matter how long I live on the sea."

"How long have you lived here?" Paul asked.

Romero returned with another chair, this one painted blue. "How long is it, Rom, six years or seven we've been here?"

"Eight. I think eight now."

Romero unscrewed the cap from the bottle of white wine and poured his wife a full glass. "You would prefer red or white?" he asked Paul. His accent was Spanish, Paul thought, or possibly Italian.

"White with fish is excellent. Thanks."

Romero filled Paul's glass and poured himself a glass of red. "Red is excellent with everything," he said, raising his glass in a toast. "Salud!"

When they'd polished off both the white and red wine, Romero produced a bottle of Bundaberg spiced rum from his bag. Georgiana referred to it as *Bundy* saying it was as close to a national spirit as Australia possessed. It tasted of caramel and molasses and, oddly enough, banana?

"Do I detect banana in here?" Paul asked.

"There aren't bananas in the mix, I don't believe, but you wouldn't be the first person to taste them," Georgiana said.

Paul took another sip of the sweet, amber fire. "I'm not a rum drinker, but I like this one."

All evening, he kept the conversation focused on his guests, learning that Romero originated from Spain and the two of them met while backpacking around North America in their early twenties. The experience of the hostels and backpacker hotels during their travels inspired them to turn an inherited family vacation property into a home away from home for travellers. They'd been together for ten years but married only one, waiting until there was enough money saved to bring Romero's family to Australia for the wedding. Paul knew about their parents, their siblings, their childhoods, and the history of the hotel at Nambucca Heads. He was running out of questions.

"So, Paul, what brings you down under?" Georgiana asked.

And there it was. The first question leading down a path he had no desire to tread. It had been such a lovely, and normal, evening.

"I came with a friend who's starring in a movie being filmed here. Do you know of Mark Jeffery?"

Georgiana put a hand on Paul's shoulder, her eyes wide. "You're mates with Mark Jeffery? You can't be serious."

"But I am. Went to school together. Friends ever since."

The conversation turned to the experience of being the close friend of a celebrity. It wasn't always easy to walk in Mark's shadow, but his fame could be a handy diversion from unwelcome questions.

The full moon hung high in the night sky by the time Paul's dinner guests retired to their suite in the main hotel. Despite the many glasses of wine and rum, Paul was far from ready for bed. He kicked off his shoes, rolled up his pant legs and walked to the water's edge. The full moon illuminated the ocean, creating glistening waves that carried silver foam to his bare feet. Breathtaking. Despite being all alone on the beach, the negative thoughts and images didn't come. For the first time since that life-changing trip up the stairs of his flat six weeks earlier, Paul felt he just might make it through the hell he'd been living.

Gazing up at the clear, starlit night, he located the iconic Southern Cross. Although decades since he'd last heard the

Crosby, Stills and Nash song, the lyrics came easily. Singing to himself as he sauntered through the waves, he kicked the glittering water into the night sky. A mere flicker, but it was there, the promise of the coming day.

When Paul booked the neighbouring cabana for Mark, Georgiana was beside herself with excitement. "Mark f'ing Jeffery coming to stay at our little hotel," was how she'd put it.

Mark had three days between shoots and said he wanted to spend some "seaside time with his best mate." Paul assumed his friend would want to go back to the resort at Coffs Harbour, but he'd surprised him with his willingness to sleep in a cabana smaller than the bedroom closet in his London home … and walk the path to a shared loo.

The door to Mark's cabana hung open and Paul found Georgiana placing a small vase of flowers on the nightstand.

"I didn't get flowers." Paul stood in the doorway, leaning on the frame.

Georgiana nearly dropped the vase and whirled. "You startled me." Her face flushed and her eyes went to the flowers in her hand. "I was just … trying … to make things … nice … for our guest."

Paul chuckled. "It's okay. I can pick my own flowers."

"It's only that we've not had anyone remotely famous stay here and, well, *Mark Jeffery*." Her large eyes threatened to pop from her face.

"He's really rather ordinary, you know. Just a British bloke like me, with more money and fame and good looks. And hair. All that annoying thick hair."

Georgiana placed the flowers on the bright yellow bedside table. "Do you think he'll be comfortable in here? I'm sure it's not what he's used to."

"He'll be fine. We were in Scouts as boys and he was a far better camper than I."

She tugged at the bedspread, removing a wrinkle.

"Stop fussing. He'll be fine. He said he was looking forward to getting away from *it*. And by it he means the stuff of his life. This will be perfect."

"Charming." Mark was squinting at the hotel and its small, colourful cabanas. He'd arrived by taxi in the late afternoon and he and Paul were enjoying a beer at Paul's outdoor table. "And the owners seem agreeable. She raved about the dinner you prepared."

"I'm guessing that's a hint for a re-invite while you're staying. She's rather a fan, and a mite rattled by your being here."

"That would explain the averting of eyes, providing the wrong key, and neglecting to return my credit card until reminded … twice."

"Georgiana is kind and they've been gracious hosts. If you're okay with it, I'll invite them round. She'd love it."

"But not tonight. I've made all the polite chitchat I can manage for a day or two." Mark took a drink from his beer. "And how are you doing? You're looking better, less like a Basset."

"Well, that's something. I believe I've turned a corner or, at least, I can now see the corner," he pointed, "just ahead there."

"That's good. Happy to hear it. Are you coming back to Sydney soon? I've missed you."

"That's not true and you needn't say it. We've been friends a long time and I'm well aware of your love of solitude when working."

"But I also enjoy your company."

Paul's eyes shifted to the surf, rolling in as it always did: rhythmically, reliably. "You've been a tremendous support these past eight weeks, and I am ever so grateful, but it's time for me to blaze my own trail."

"To where?"

"Not England, that much I know. The owners here spent six months touring in America. It's rather appealing. I'd not been out of the UK before I came to Australia with you and I think I might have the bug, the travel bug. At my age. Can you imagine?"

"There's no right age to see the world. We just do it when we're very young and very old because that's when we have the most time. I'd say forty-four is the perfect age to travel. Enough life experience to know what you like and don't so you won't waste a bunch of time and money sorting that out. And, you have friends with the wherewithal to assist."

"Oh no. That's where I draw the line. I expect there'll be some kind of settlement from my well-employed, cheating wife and that should keep me fed and housed until I unpack my suitcase somewhere."

"Somewhere? You're not planning to return to the UK?"

"I likely will. It's home. But not London. Too much history. And not enough sea … or sky."

Mark leaned back in his chair, eyes scanning the distant horizon where darkening sky met water. "Now that I understand. But you *will* let me help you. Travelling is not inexpensive these days, and it may be some time before there's anything from Rachel. Divorce proceedings are slow business."

Paul peered down the neck of his beer bottle. "Divorce."

"Oh. Isn't that what you meant by settlement?"

"Yes, of course. I just hadn't used the big 'D' word yet. It's difficult to imagine myself as divorced, having an ex-wife. I married for life."

"But she didn't. I'm sorry."

"Me as well."

Seven

Despite her abrupt departure the previous night, Sandra returned for Ian's second appearance on the Pablo's stage. She came dressed in Baja-appropriate attire this time—sandals and short trousers—and her shoulder-length hair rested in a loose bun at the nape of her neck.

Paul met her at the entrance. "Good evening. Happy to see you've returned for a second serving of our new minstrel. Where would you like to sit?" Paul gestured to the many empty tables and stools. "As you can see, there are plenty of options."

"I'll take that same stool at the bar."

"Excellent choice. And dining or just drinking? Or neither is fine. You're welcome to sit and enjoy the music." On the heels of her abrupt departure the previous night, Paul wanted her to feel complete freedom, no pressure, worried she might turn and run if he said the wrong thing. There'd been a lot of running during the early months after Rachel and healing only took place when he could sit still for a time.

"I had a late lunch in La Paz today, but maybe something light. A salad?"

"Did you go shopping for new vacation clothes?"

Sandra looked down at her attire and ran hands along her thighs. "Yeah. Jeans were not the thing for Baja. And my feet ached to get out of closed-toed shoes. When I left home I wasn't planning to be … well … I didn't pack very well."

Paul followed Sandra to her stool and handed her a menu. "You'll find two salads on the menu, a Caesar and a house. I'm rather partial to the house, local greens with—"

"I'm sure it's delicious, like everything else you make. The food here is fabulous. I'm sorry I haven't mentioned it before now. Are you the chef?"

"I am *the* chef, but not *a* chef, if you catch my meaning. And Carmelita is excellent help. Have you met her?"

"Yes. She brought me clean towels yesterday. Is she your wife?"

"Oh, no. I don't have a wife. Anymore. She … my ex … is back in London." Sandra remained quiet, waiting for him to say more. "Did you enjoy La Paz?" Paul asked.

"I did. Plenty of great shops and restaurants. But much busier than your tiny village."

"Indeed. I do as much shopping as possible in San Leandro but still need to schedule a weekly excursion to the city." He hesitated, glancing down at Sandra's new footwear—flip-flop style, with engraved flowers parading across the instep strap. "If you ever want to go again, you're welcome to ride along. The road can be, well, you know, you drove it."

"Thanks. But I'm fine. I've always liked to explore off the beaten path."

"Hence showing up here."

He'd made her smile. For the moment, his work was done. "Well, I'd best get to the grill. We'll be busy once the music starts." Paul took two steps toward the kitchen before turning back. "I'm sorry. Did you want something to drink?" The focus on helping Sandra was distracting him from his duties as a host.

"I shouldn't, but that vat of margarita last night …"

"And why shouldn't you?"

She smiled, again. "Well, now that you mention it, no good reason."

"Precisely. This is Mexico. We frown on shoulds down here, rules of any sort really."

"Then one margarita, on the rocks, lots of salt."

By the time Ian neared the end of his first set, the restaurant was full and it was all Paul could do to keep up with orders. Carmelita ran between working the bar, helping Elena on the floor, and assisting Paul in the kitchen. Arturo bussed tables and washed dishes. They performed like a well-rehearsed stage show, each one entering and exiting on cue, everyone remembering their lines and feeding off each other's energy. He hadn't thought of it in this way before, but Pablo's was his new stage, and tonight's capacity crowd an opportunity to bring down the house.

They had come close in the months since he'd opened, but this was the first time they'd filled every table and every seat at the bar. There were even people standing along the back wall enjoying a drink and the music. Pablo's was a success.

Alone in the kitchen, Paul spun on one foot, taking a bow before returning to the stovetop to flip each fillet of snapper.

"Señor?"

Arturo was standing in the doorway. Paul felt his face flush "Arturo, my man. May I just say that you are doing a superb job? Thanks for your help tonight."

"My mother is having some trouble keeping up with the bar. Would you like me to assist her?"

"I would love that, but your age is a problem, as is Elena's."

The young man's face fell.

"But, in two years, if you still want it, the bar is yours."

Elena clipped two more orders to the ticket wheel. "Two more specials."

"I'm running out of snapper. Do all the tables have their meal orders in?"

"All but one." Elena said, "There is a table of four still drinking cocktails."

"Well, hopefully no more than two guests order the special. The reservations didn't suggest a full house." Paul plated the orders of ginger-lime fish he'd been cooking and Elena disappeared with them out the kitchen door.

"Can you tidy up in here while I tend the bar?" Paul asked Arturo.

Despite the disappointment Paul knew he must feel, Arturo only smiled and nodded. For such a young man, he was very professional and a great addition to Casa del Mar Azul.

He clapped a hand on Arturo's back. "*Gracias*. You're the best, Amigo."

Ian was deep in conversation with Sandra when Paul took his place behind the bar. Even when you've run *away from home*, speaking to someone *from home* was a comfort. That he remembered. After leaving Mark behind in Australia, he'd often sought the company of other Brits, usually over drinks in a pub, and those little pieces of home made it easier to stay on the road.

Paul had to admit to feeling envious. He'd wanted to be the one to help this woman find her way back to the living, like it might somehow repay the universe for its support when his life had fallen down around him. But who helped her wasn't important, only that she got the help she needed. To be out two nights in a row and shopping in La Paz today were definite signs of progress.

"Ah, and here is our gracious host now." Ian waved Paul over. "This place is rocking! Is this a typical Saturday night?"

"When you say typical, are you referring to past or future Saturdays?"

Ian laughed. "To the future." He raised an empty hand.

"You don't have a drink."

"Your staff seem so busy, I didn't want to bother them."

"Well, who better to bother than the owner? What can I get you?"

"Just a beer. Any label of Mexican makes me happy."

Paul pulled a Sol from the cooler, popped the top off and set it in front of Ian.

The drink orders kept arriving, from Elena, from Carmelita, and Paul stayed busy behind the bar. He attempted to eavesdrop on Ian and Sandra, but she had her back to him and he could only hear Ian's side of the discussion. Paul feared the Canadian might ask the wrong questions again and send Sandra retreating to her room, but he stayed with small talk about Baja, sharing stories of his Cabo adventures. Sounded like it had been quite the party for a while, but Ian was now content in San Leandro and hoping to make a go of it in the area. That was good news. Paul would love to assist Ian in "making a go of it" if that meant regular appearances in Pablo's. A packed house with the drinks flowing and no one in a hurry to leave. Paul's dream was becoming a reality.

And he couldn't have done it without Mark Jeffery.

Eight

Canyonlands National Park, Utah, USA

Paul stepped out on the rough wooden deck of his rented yurt. Accommodations other than sticks and bricks while visiting one of America's national parks seemed essential. His preference would have been one of the many campgrounds right in the park, but the weather was turning cold for sleeping in his 4Runner. There'd been a dusting of snow the previous night.

The canopy of stars overhead took his breath away, breath visible in the chilly night air. Growing up in London and spending most of his life there, he'd not had much opportunity to stargaze outside of infrequent visits to an uncle's farm.

Paul tugged the front of his jacket closed and zipped it up, brushed the dusting of snow from a wooden deck chair, and sat.

Three months earlier, he'd flown from Sydney to Los Angeles, but it seemed much longer ago. Time on the road slowed to a tortoise pace, the days filled with new sites and experiences, the evenings long and leisurely.

After Mark's visit to Nambucca Heads, Paul had spent two more weeks with Georgiana and Romero, picking their brains on travelling in America, before returning to Sydney for a few days with Mark. His friend worried about him setting off alone. It was true, Paul had never been a solitude kind of guy, but this was different. A soul's journey was better taken by one.

He shivered and crossed his arms over his chest, burying his hands in his armpits. The wooden chair felt like a block of ice underneath him. But it was too beautiful a night to be indoors. He quickly stepped inside to retrieve the barbecue lighter and a blanket and then ignited the gas firepit which occupied the middle of the round deck. He dragged his chair closer to the fire, spread the blanket over it, and settled in again.

Mark was partly right about Paul and solitude, he had been lonely. He and Mark spoke weekly and texted more often, he'd called each of his four siblings and his parents at least once, met a few fellow travellers at the more communal-style accommodations, but, mostly, he spent his days alone, learning to enjoy his own company. Much to his surprise, he rather did. He'd decided he wasn't such a bad bloke, just a little lost.

Somewhere on the road, Paul spotted a bumper sticker that read, "We travel not to escape life, but for life to not escape us." He'd started off seeking to escape, but it had shifted after about a month and for the past two he'd been soaking up every new place and experience.

His old 4Runner, *the Beast*, he'd bought with money borrowed from Mark and then driven straight up the west coast of North America. One spectacular scene unfolded into another and another. Between driving on the wrong side of the road and gawking at the scenery, he'd been a hazard to himself and others in those early weeks.

He'd not intended to visit Canada but, once he'd driven as far as Bellingham, Washington, it seemed foolish not to continue. Who knew when he'd have another chance. With little knowledge of the country beyond its notorious winter weather, he worried about Canadian summer nearing its end, but the locals assured him he'd have reasonable temperatures through September and even into October. If not for the lateness of the season, he might have continued northward. He felt an inexplicable urge to drive until the road ended and stay for a time. But, when he searched it on Google Maps and observed the endless highway as it etched its passage through the continent, he swung east instead. The road north would have to wait.

Throughout British Columbia and into Alberta, Paul came face to face with nature's mind-blowing beauty. And life, so much life: elk, deer, moose, bighorn sheep, mountain goats, black and grizzly bears. Paul created a wildlife bucket list and he'd almost checked off every box by the time he left Banff National Park. Only the cougar and beaver remained, and a park ranger advised him to abandon the notion of seeking out the elusive and predatory cougar.

Jasper National Park was the first dark sky preserve he encountered. He hadn't known such a thing existed. Once he'd done a bit of online research and found a list, he had another set of boxes to check off.

The dark sky of the Cypress Hills drew him onto Canada's vast prairie, where he was astounded by the space, the enormous sky, and an unimaginable quiet. The Cypress Hills were where he ran into the first snow and decided it was time to head south.

And south took him to Yellowstone Park, where he checked bison off his wildlife list and experienced his first yurt, before joining the Interstate 15 highway through Idaho and into Utah. Canyonlands National Park was on his American dark sky preserves hit list.

Paul looked up at the sky and its spray of a million stars. The vastness of the North American landscape was matched only by its skies.

His cell phone vibrated in his coat pocket. He pulled it out and there she was on the screen. Rachel. They hadn't been in contact since he'd left London. He stared at her smiling face, a photo he'd taken when they'd holidayed at Bath the year before. When they'd been happy. Or, at least, he was happy, or thought he was. Funny how one event could change the colour of all those that had gone before. Would she have been seeing Jeremy already then?

For months he'd waited for a call, hoping that somehow all of this would end in life going back to normal. Normal. If life in London with an unfaithful wife and a failing career was normal, did he want that? This time, this trip, had changed him. The thought of returning to *that life* felt … suffocating, defeating. His finger hovered over the green button … too long. The call went to voicemail.

Nine

Puerto Peñasco (Rocky Point), Sonora, Mexico

Arizona was an adventurer's feast from the spiritual energy centres of Sedona to the indescribable size of the Grand Canyon to the unique flora and fauna of the Sonoran desert. Paul had found a new love and her name was desert, but he missed the water.

He planned to return to California and its coast until he strayed into a tiny town called Ajo where many of his fellow campers were preparing for the short journey to Puerto Peñasco, Mexico, otherwise known as Rocky Point. Puerto Peñasco rested on the shores of the Sea of Cortez. The sea, and another international boundary, beckoned.

Two weeks into Paul's time in Mexico, fate pointed him down the path of his next adventure, when he met Rod and Melinda, Americans who were visiting friends in Puerto Peñasco, friends originally from the UK.

It had been weeks since Paul had encountered anyone from "the homeland" and, when British accents reached his ears from the table next to his in the hotel restaurant, he couldn't stop himself. As soon as there was a lull in their conversation, he turned toward the group of four. "Hello. Sorry to bust in but I couldn't help but catch your accents. Are you from London?"

The red-haired woman smiled at him and answered, "Yes. Southfields."

Paul spun in his chair. "I grew up in Southfields."

The woman was in her late sixties or early seventies and wore heavy turquoise jewelry around her tanned neck and wrists. "A pleasure to meet you. I'm Carolyn and this is my husband, Edward. He's from the north but I long ago civilized him."

Edward extended a hand. "Good to meet you."

"I'm Paul, Paul Hutchings. Again, I apologize for interrupting, I've been abroad a long while and the familiar sound of central London was irresistible."

"Not at all," said Carolyn. "We left London years ago, and it's always lovely to meet someone from home. You're on holiday?"

"An extended version. I left London almost six months ago."

Edward leaned toward the other man at the table and they exchanged words.

Just as Carolyn opened her mouth to speak, Edward interjected. "You're welcome to join us. Always room for another at our table. These are our friends, Rod and Melinda, from across the water."

Paul stood and shook hands with the other couple. They appeared a little older than their British companions, but fit looking.

"Across the water? So, Europe?"

Rod laughed, a big sound, audible to everyone in the restaurant, and possibly those out on the street. "No, not that water. We're right about …" He pointed out to the sea, sliding his aim right and left. "There." He'd landed on a location to the southwest. "San Leandro. A tiny place you've probably never heard of and are even less likely to have visited." His speech carried the telltale drawl of the American accent, slight in his case but very audible in the way he spoke his o's and a's.

"But charming and idyllic," Carolyn cut in. And back to central London. Studying accents had been one of Paul's favourite parts of learning the art of acting.

Carolyn and Rod made a space between them and Paul pulled a chair from the neighbouring table. "Thank you for the invitation. I won't bore you with tales of my many lonely days on the road but, suffice to say, I welcome the company."

"And what brings you to Mexico?" Rod asked, his . "Business? Pleasure? Witness protection?" The big man's face was serious, but his eyes danced with humour. Paul liked him immediately.

"Nothing so exciting. I met some Mexico-bound RVers in Arizona and they encouraged me to tag along, talked at length about the beauty of the Sea of Cortez. I was California bound, but they assured me it was cheaper in Mexico and that I'd love the food. Both true. That, and a fourth stamp in my passport."

"Speaking of loving the food," Melinda said, "maybe we should order some before I begin chewing on my napkin?" She was quieter spoken than her husband, but with a similar brightness in her eyes. She was one of those women who went grey with elegance, her hair cut Judi-Dench short.

Rod called the server over and they placed their orders. Melinda requested a dish called chile rellenos, not something Paul had tried, and he followed suit.

"You'll love it," Melinda said. "It's my absolute favourite Mexican dish."

Edward and Carolyn were ex-pats who lived in Washington State during the summer and Puerto Peñasco when, as they put it, the autumn rains arrived. Edward had transferred from London to Seattle in the latter part of his career and, when he retired, they stayed. Tired of the chill, damp winters of their entire lives to that point, they sought out a sunny winter home, settling in northern Mexico. They chose Puerto Peñasco for its proximity to both the water and the United States border.

"And what do you and Melinda do in the idyllic village of San Leandro?" Paul asked.

Before Rod could answer, Melinda replied, "Work too much."

Rod rolled his eyes. "My wife would like me to retire."

"Yes. Again." She leaned toward Paul across the table. "He retired from our business over ten years ago and we moved to Mexico … to relax."

"I do relax. Pescadero Palms is my relaxation." Turning to Paul, he said, "We run a small hotel. San Leandro is a big fishing area so we get a lot of fishermen. I've always loved to fish and, while I was working, rarely had the time."

"He goes fishing with the guests and I'm left to look after the hotel."

"Don't listen to her. There's help."

"You call that help?" Melinda turned to Paul. "Our daughter and her husband were quick to sign up when we bought the hotel and needed staff. But they spend more time on the beach than working. Help, my ass."

The table went quiet.

Paul was feeling like he'd landed in the middle of something and wasn't sure how to proceed. Perhaps a joke to lighten the mood?

And then Melinda's face split into a grin and Rod started to laugh.

Carolyn shook her head. "They do this frequently, mock battling. You've done well to stay in your chair. They've frightened off more than one new acquaintance."

"I hope that wasn't the intent," Paul said. He was a tad serious. How was he to take these two Americans?

Rod laughed louder. "No, not this time, but it's proven a helpful strategy in the past. Do you remember the last time we were here, Edward, that obnoxious Texan who kept showing up every time we sat down to eat a meal? Skittered away at the first sign of a domestic scene." Rod raised a glass. "To our new friend from England, who's passed the first test."

Paul couldn't help but wonder what test number two would be.

Carolyn and Edward invited Paul to their home for dinner the next evening. They lived in a thousand-square-foot single-storey house in an area called Cholla Bay. It was a simple property, with nothing but sand for a front yard, but had a view of the sea from what they called the *margarita deck* on the rooftop.

Rod and Melinda were staying in the guest room and Paul found the four of them on the rooftop when he arrived. Carolyn was at the railing waving him up as soon as he stepped from the taxi.

"Come up. Come up. It's time for foursies. The drinks are cold and the sun is warm." She pointed to the stairway on the building's south side.

"Brilliant," Paul said when he reached the top. Rooftop patios were a favourite of his. "What a terrific spot."

"Margarita or cerveza?" Carolyn asked.

"Do they both qualify as," he made bunny ears with his fingers, "*foursies?*"

"Oh yes."

"Well, margarita then. And precisely what is *foursies?*"

Carolyn chuckled. "It's a term we picked up from the RV people. With the border less than two hours from here, we've met several snowbirds in their motorhomes and caravans. They refer to their afternoon cocktails and snacks as foursies. It's a thing, apparently. So we've adopted it. Foursies on the margarita deck." She handed Paul his drink. "Help yourself to the food."

The table held bowls and platters of smoked fish, cheese, crackers, and the Mexican staple, tortilla chips with a fresh salsa.

"So, Paul, we've been talking," Rod said, "and we think—"

"Let the man sit down and get a bite of food, Rod," Melinda cut in.

"Fine. Sit. Eat. And then I have a proposition for you."

———

The conversation turned to news of the area, most notably the hurricane far out at sea with the potential to make landfall in Baja. Rod's concern for their hotel was evident, and they'd made plans to return the next day.

"Which brings me to," Rod said, "we think you should come with us. You mentioned you were running low on travel funds and, as my wife communicated so clearly last night," he blew her a kiss, "we can use some help around the place, especially with this storm potentially coming ashore in our area. We can't offer much in terms of a wage but you'd have a room at the hotel while you're there and we can set you up with a grill and a small fridge."

"Oh. Well." Paul had no words. These people knew almost nothing of him after just one day, and yet here they were offering him a job and a place to live. The American people had been friendly throughout his travels, but this seemed exceptional.

"It would just be a temporary role, helping me catch up on some maintenance. My son-in-law is about as handy as a—"

"Rod," Melinda said.

"Fine. He's not very ... mechanically ... inclined, let's just say. Yesterday, you mentioned the renovations on your London apartment and I wondered if you might like to visit our fair peninsula, extend your travel fund a few weeks. It's desert, like this, but the sea is right on our doorstep in all its blue Cortez glory."

As had been happening frequently on his journey, every time Paul arrived at what he saw as the end of a road, there'd be a sign pointing in a new and unexpected direction. Constantly being on the move had become tiring, and a place to call home, one with purpose, seemed too good to be true. The initial novelty of moving through the world as observer rather than participant had worn off and Paul needed to apply himself to something, contribute.

"The desert has grown on me in unexpected ways, and I've always loved the sea. It sounds, well, perfect, to be quite frank.

I accept." Paul stood and extended a hand and Rod grabbed it and gave a firm shake.

"There, Melinda. Two birds with one stone," Rod said.

Paul opened his mouth but before he could ask the question Rod said, "My dearest wife would like me to work less, as she may have mentioned, and she also likes to help people, a bit of a collector of strays."

"Rod!" Melinda's reddening face turned to Paul. "I don't see you as a stray, only thought you might enjoy having a home for a while. I know I always do when we've been travelling for any length of time."

"Thank you. And you're correct, including the stray part."

Rod raised a glass to Paul for the second time since they'd met, "Since you'll be working under the radar of the Mexican authorities, we'll just call you Pablo. To Pablo, our new … director of restorations!"

Amid the laughter that followed, Paul realized he had no idea how to get himself and his 4Runner from one side of the Sea of Cortez to the other, and in the path of a hurricane.

Ten

What Paul expected to be a two-car convoy to Rod and Melinda's hotel turned into a solo expedition. They'd flown with a friend in his small, private plane and, although they had space for Paul and one bag, he was reluctant to leave *The Beast* behind. The path marched ever forward, and he didn't wish to be without transportation when the next leg of his journey presented itself.

The trip to San Leandro would take twenty-plus hours if he travelled counter-clockwise around the Sea of Cortez. On Edward's recommendation, Paul opted to take the clockwise route, an eleven-hour drive to Topolobampo followed by a seven-hour ferry trip. The travel time would be almost the same, including embarking and disembarking the ferry, but he could relax once they'd set sail, and Paul loved being on the water.

Rod advised him to monitor the weather, stay inland where possible. The forecasters expected the hurricane to make landfall in the far south of Mexico, but that was still speculation.

When Paul left Puerto Peñasco, the clear, blue sky gave no indication of threatening weather and the route took him away from the coast after Puerto Libertad. Rod would be pleased. A Mexican road was quite a different experience from the interstate highways north of the border, plus he didn't get the early start he intended, but he made excellent time nonetheless, reaching Guaymas before dark.

The small city of Guaymas sat right on the Sea of Cortez and, despite Rod's concerns about being near the coast, Paul just couldn't stay away. The hurricane would be more dangerous near the sea, but it might be Paul's one and only opportunity to experience a tropical storm. If the hurricane altered its current path and Guaymas fell in line for a direct hit, he'd retreat inland.

The young woman working behind the desk of the Bahia Beaches Motel knew enough English to ask Paul if he was aware of the approaching storm. When he said yes, and that he planned to stay anyway, she gave him a printed notice prepared by the local authorities. They were advising tourists to evacuate coastal areas and seek accommodations inland. But he wasn't afraid. Could any weather system have the power to upend his life like Rachel had? Hurricane Rachel. Paul smiled to himself as he filled out the registration form.

Settled into his room for the night, Paul emailed Rod and Melinda, letting them know he was delayed because of the weather. The hurricane had strengthened through the day, and they predicted it would make landfall early the next morning. When he'd called the Baja Ferry office, he'd been told that they had suspended all sailings until the hurricane had passed. If they didn't sustain any damage to their ferries or docks, service would resume in two days.

Paul switched on the television. All channels were in Spanish, but understanding the language wasn't necessary to interpret the weather map with the massive, swirling cloud off the coast of Guatemala. The meteorologist displayed dotted lines on the map showing the storm's most likely path and possible deviations. One of the alternate routes would bring it right to Guaymas.

That was a fresh development.

Everything he'd seen before now projected landfall much farther south. Opening three different weather apps, he viewed three different projections of which way the storm would track. In two, he was safe, but in the third, things might get wild at his little motel. Paul stared at the weather map on his phone. Damn. He'd wanted to stay close to the sea, had ignored Rod's advice, and now it was ten o'clock and the hurricane threatened to change course.

He opened Google Maps. Almost two hours to Ciudad Obregón, the first-day destination recommended by Carolyn. He could be there by midnight. Paul set his overnight bag on the bed and began stuffing in items he'd scattered about the room—a book, his bathroom kit, a water bottle—his heart rate increasing as he packed. He zipped up the bag and opened the door to his room, stepping out into the warm evening. A whisper of breeze carried the smell of the sea from two blocks away. He'd planned to walk the beach in the morning, even if it was raining, and visit the El Salado Estuary as soon as the storm passed. The website said the estuary was home to over one hundred species of birds.

Paul gazed up at the shrouded sky, peach street lights reflecting off the clouds.

It was as though his life had turned into a game of cat and mouse with him playing the mouse. He'd been chased from the best role of his career by a second cousin's son, or some such thing, of the producer. He could have fought it. They had a contract. But he walked away.

Some guy named Jeremy had chased him from his own home and bed. He should have hit the guy, yelled and screamed, ordered him out of his house. But he left peacefully.

London became uncomfortable, so he got on a plane.

Feeling like a third wheel in Sydney with Mark and his friends, he hopped a train.

And, ever since he'd flown from Australia to America, he'd kept moving, staying nowhere long enough for the discomfort of his life to catch up with him.

Paul stepped back inside his room and dropped his bag on a chair. He'd chosen this place to stay the night, to weather the storm. This time he would stand his ground.

———

Paul awoke to the sound of wind rattling the shutters and shingles. He reached for the lamp, but no light illuminated the room when he turned the switch. Which also meant there would be no television to report on the storm's status. He powered up his phone and waited for the chime, indicating it was open for business. The Weather Channel reports showed the storm had dropped to a category two before making landfall and was still far to the south. What he was hearing must be the fringes of the system, ruffling the Mexican coast. There would be rain, some wind, and no power for a time, but the roof wouldn't come down on his head before the sun came up, and his destination, Rod's Baja hotel, would still be standing when he got there.

Paul climbed out of bed and dragged the drapes aside, squinting into the blackness. Other than rain splattering against the window, he saw only his reflection. He looked into the eyes staring at him from the glass, the lack of light turning them from blue to black. They were the eyes of a survivor. He could have retreated inland, but he'd stayed the course.

And, if he were fair, back in London, he'd set out to discover the world, instead of holing up in a sad little flat. Paul smiled at the man in the window. He might be a runner, but he was gaining ground on what almost felt like … joy.

Back in bed, Paul stared up at the ceiling, the light from his phone casting a blue-ish glow on the stucco. The sun would come up in a few hours, and he would find a cup of coffee, walk the beach, visit the birds, do the things he'd come here to do. No matter how dark the night, the sun could be counted on to rise.

Eleven

Paul hesitated at the door to Sandra's room, his fist raised, hating to do it.

He hadn't run across his Canadian guest for two days, since Saturday night when Ian played in Pablo's. He prided himself on leaving his guests to their own, but he was concerned about this one.

Sandra had remained at the bar through Ian's second set and beyond, laughing and chatting with her fellow Canadian until past midnight. She'd seemed cheerful, normal, so not like the shell of a human he'd welcomed on arrival. It pleased Paul to see it, had him humming *Don't Worry, Be Happy* (Ian's last song for the night) all the way back to his suite.

He'd hoped, and rather expected, that she'd come for breakfast on the patio Sunday morning or today, but no sign of her. And no dinner order last night. The hotel had been busy, granted, but Mar Azul was a small place, making it difficult to *not* encounter his guests many times each day.

He knocked.

No response from inside.

He banged on the door, thinking he might at least rouse the little dog.

Nothing.

Carmelita said she'd delivered fresh towels on Sunday morning and Sandra had said she'd be fine until mid-week. Paul appreciated low-maintenance guests but, in this case, he'd have preferred someone visiting her room each day. Although tempted to enter, he would check the beach first. Her Toyota sat parked in the side lot so she couldn't be too far off.

Paul fetched the binoculars from his suite and climbed to the rooftop patio. When he'd first purchased Rod's Pescadero Palms, it had three deck areas. The lower level next to the beach was the largest and the space he'd turned into Pablo's; the second level, off the south side, housed the dual-purpose breakfast-in-the-morning and sunbathing-in-the-afternoon patio; and on the rooftop was the third deck area, open for celebrations and other special events or just sitting and enjoying the view. The artists loved it as a painting location.

Paul pulled a chair up to the railing and scanned the beach with his binoculars. It was a beautiful afternoon with only a light breeze, so finding one average-sized woman dressed in vacation attire amongst the many beach goers would not be easy. Paul searched for a small, wiry dog instead. Sandra mentioned Rufus loved to chase the waves, so he searched the space where water met sand. And, bingo, there was the terrier, jumping at the leading foam and dashing away before water touched his belly.

But not a soul occupied the beach nearby. Paul shifted his gaze to the water. Nothing. He stood and squinted into the binoculars, willing his eyes to locate a woman swimming in the surf. He glimpsed red and focused on that area. The waves blocked his view, making it challenging to see anything for more than an instant. There it was again, a flash of red, but no sign of arms swinging or legs kicking.

Adrenaline shot through Paul's veins and he bolted down the stairs and around the hotel to the beach. This couldn't be happening. It was a trick of the light and the water, making it appear that someone in a red swimsuit bobbed in the surf, drifting away from shore with the Pacific's tidal flow.

As he got closer, Paul heard Rufus barking, and realized the little dog wasn't chasing waves but barking at the sea, for his mistress. *Bloody hell.* When the dog caught sight of Paul, he ran toward him, tail wagging, and then jumped up, once, twice, three times, leaving sandy paw prints on Paul's trouser leg.

Paul gave the dog's head a quick rub. "Hey, little guy. Where is she? Help me find her." He raised the binoculars to his eyes and Rufus returned to jumping at the waves and barking.

It was more difficult to see anything from beach level. He needed a spotter on the rooftop with a radio. But that would take too much time. Rufus continued at the water's edge, fifty feet away, barking at the moving water.

Paul scanned the sea straight out from the dog's location. And there it was, the red flash. "Good boy, Rufus."

He dropped the binoculars in the sand, stripped down to his boxers and headed into the surf. He'd been swimming in the Sea of Cortez since he'd first come to Baja and felt confident in his ability to navigate the sometimes treacherous currents. Although twenty degrees Celsius, the water felt like ice to Paul's adrenaline-filled body, and he inhaled sharply when it reached his midsection. Ignoring the shock, he dove in, propelling himself forward with a strong pull of his arms.

Every minute or two, he'd stop swimming and scan the surrounding waves, treading water. The sounds of the sea had absorbed Rufus' barking. *Damn it, Sandra. Where are you?*

There. A flicker of red in the distance, before it vanished behind another wave. And again, the red.

Paul swam toward the flash of colour. His arms were tiring, but the fight-or-flight effect of the adrenaline fired his muscles and lungs. He stopped and located the red swimsuit again. He couldn't tell if she floated face up or down, but it was obvious she wasn't swimming or trying to return to shore. "Sandra!" he shouted. "Ms. Lyall!"

No response.

He started swimming again. *No. Don't let this happen.* She was stronger than this, wasn't she?

He'd discovered his own strength, his own will to live, in this very sea. Although not a religious man, as he swam, Paul prayed the same would be true for Sandra Lyall.

Twelve

Paul's initial week at Rod and Melinda's Baja hotel had been full. He'd forgotten how satisfying it felt to be productive, to help, to put his hands to work. And, thanks to his efforts, the hotel's blue trim had a fresh coat of paint, including the shutters, the window frames, and the guest-room doors.

The fifteen-room lodging sat seaside, its Mediterranean blue-on-white colour scheme a perfect fit in the surroundings. The moment he saw the place, glowing white against the blue of Cortez, Paul was charmed. He'd wound his way down the drive through the desert flora he'd come to love: the cacti, the scruffy shrubs, the trees with green bark that he kept meaning to inquire about. Pescadero Palms was an oasis, complete with a pair of palm trees next to the building.

The McCraes, Rod and Melinda, had owned the small resort for sixteen years. Purchased as an investment, it became a retirement project when they left their respective careers, he as a business owner and she a nurse. Rod loved the place and spent most of his time puttering around or taking guests out fishing. Melinda worked in the front office every morning, managing any checkouts and organizing things for the day, leaving their daughter, Wendy, and her husband with the cleaning and afternoon arrivals. It was an easy day for Melinda but, based on her comments to Paul, she would have preferred to be reading a book or working in her garden. At seventy-two, she was ready for complete retirement.

Paul washed the paint from his hands and changed into a clean pair of shorts and a t-shirt. He and Rod had taken to wrapping up each day on the beach out front of the hotel. Rod sat, cooler bag at his side and beer in hand, when Paul's bare feet reached the warm sand.

"Hey," Paul called as he approached.

Rod turned and raised his bottle in Paul's direction, Maui Jim knockoffs perched on his nose.

"It's going to be a nice evening. But then, when isn't it?" Paul dropped into the empty canvas sling chair beside Rod. "I can see why you retired here."

"If only my wife agreed with you." Rod handed Paul a chilled Baja Brewing Co ale.

"My sense is that she's just tired of working," Paul said.

"Working? She's here for two or three hours every morning."

"I think it's the *every* that might be at issue. The quantity of time is less important. I've discovered in these months of travelling that having the freedom to spend a day how one chooses is a thing to treasure."

Rod took a swallow of his beer. "But what the heck would we do if we weren't here?"

"Couldn't you be here in Baja but hire someone to manage the hotel?"

"That would never work for me. I've run my own business far too long, had half a dozen hardware stores in Michigan. Every store had a manager, but I still spent time in each location every week. It's my way. You don't get to be my age and not know what makes you tick."

"Wasn't it tough to part with your stores, not knowing what a new owner might do?"

"Strangely enough, not so much. Once they weren't mine anymore, it didn't seem to matter. In fact, I heard two of the locations went under and, although I feel bad for the owners, they're no longer my responsibility. I signed the sale documents and walked away."

"I suppose I can understand that. I was obsessed with my acting career, or lack thereof, until I left it behind in the UK. It's now like a closed chapter in a book I read a long time ago."

"An actor? Really. You hadn't mentioned."

"Like I said, closed chapter, and not a great one. I loved it, from my first school play as a boy, but it was time to move on."

"And what does moving on look like?" Rod asked.

"Now there lies a question I don't have an answer to."

"Seems we're in the same boat then. To our uncertain futures." Rod lifted his beer and clunked it into Paul's.

Two pale ales later, Paul retired to his room for a typical evening of reading and catching up on the news and any correspondence. He relished his daily talks with Rod. The older man was a thinker, presenting aspects of a topic Paul hadn't considered. The two men chatted about the work at the hotel, current events, a little politics. Tonight was the first time things had swung to a more personal conversation. Rod's question ran around in Paul's mind. What did *moving on* from acting look like? He hadn't realized he was finished with it until he'd spoken the words. On one hand, it freed him to give up the chase for the success that eluded him, but it also presented a monumental question. If not that, then what?

Paul picked up his phone from the table and stretched out across the bed. He hadn't checked for messages since the early morning. A text from Mark, now home in the UK, just saying hello. An email from Georgiana and Romero thanking him for the fish recipe they'd used to impress some friends. Nice.

And a voicemail from Rachel.

The last time she'd called, when he sat under the stars of Canyonlands, he'd let it go to voicemail, and then allowed a crazy idea to take root in his mind: she was calling to apologize and ask him to come home. He wanted to hear she was sorry, and she missed him, that she suffered as he did. He waited a full day to listen to her message; the fantasy taking flight. Only to have it shot down by her words. "We need to talk, Paul, about the flat, about an official separation."

And they had talked. She said she'd bought the flat and it was therefore hers, but she would pay him what she considered fair, a ten percent share. Although more than equal to what he'd contributed financially, when one considered the time he'd put into renovating and ongoing maintenance, not to mention his supporting her through law school, it was a long way from fair. He countered, she said she'd think about it and would get back to him. It had been two months.

This time he listened to her message right away, not about to repeat his mistake. There would be no fantasies of apologies or reconciliation. *Paul, it's Rachel. I've started divorce proceedings and I need to know where to send the documents. I believe you'll find the terms more than equitable. Jeremy's asked me to marry him. I want to move forward with my life.*

Paul dropped the phone to the bed and stared up at the ceiling. She wanted to marry the guy. Already. Seven months ago he went dashing up the stairs of his flat, eager to see the wife he loved, who he thought loved him back, and now she was engaged to the man he'd found her sleeping with. If only he could expunge it from his brain, the image of Rachel's face peering out at him from under her lover. To find out she'd been cheating would have been difficult no matter how it came to be, but the picture and its devastating clarity were torture. Paul rubbed his face with his hands. "Blast you. Get out!" But the image remained.

Still staring at the ceiling, he wished for a glass roof overhead to provide a view of the sky. Starry skies had been a comfort to him since that night on the beach at Nambucca Heads. He would gaze up at the vastness, the stars twinkling at him from above, and feel that things would turn out in the end, that someone, something, was on his side.

Paul dragged himself off the bed and out into the night air, wanting to scream and cry and shout to the glittering canopy overhead. He thought he'd moved on, that she couldn't hurt him anymore, but now this, now she wanted to replace him with Jeremy. An affair, a fling, a dalliance, those were survivable, but marry him, youthful Jeremy, the lawyer with the full head of hair. Paul ran his hands over his own balding scalp and dropped to his knees in the sand, the words quietly spilling from his lips as he fell. "Why wasn't I enough?"

And then the tears came, as if from faucets, pouring down his face and falling onto the sand. It had been windy all day and the roar of the surf filled his ears. He was alone. On the beach. In life.

Staggering to the water's edge, Paul waded in fully clothed. When the waves reached his chest, he dove underneath the turmoil of the surface, seeking the quiet of the depths. And he swam, pain and torment driving his arms and legs, not coming up for air until he felt his lungs would burst and then diving again for that peacefulness closer to the ocean's floor. Immersion in water blurred the mental picture he'd been struggling to erase. Was it possible to override the body's drive to breathe and just stay below, in the dark, in the calm, with that blissful blur?

No.

Rachel still held the power to inflict terrible pain, but no way would he let her end him.

His life, whatever life he could build from the rubble of his past, was up above, in the air, under the stars.

Paul was disoriented when he surfaced, the hotel not where he expected it to be. The current had carried him southeast. He was a long way from shore.

He lay on his back, looking up at the canopy of tiny lights, and then started to swim, directing himself to the closest point of land.

Thirteen

Paul was getting close. Sandra drifted fewer than twenty yards away and appeared to be face up. At least there was that. In every film he'd ever seen, dead bodies floated face down.

He swam the final distance between them, the water less tumultuous this far out. Her eyes were closed to the sun and her hands trailed in the water.

He reached for her wrist, encircling it gently with his fingers. Despite her upward position in the water, he feared she would be cold to his touch, her skin like the fish he pulled from the cooler each afternoon. But it was warm and soft in his hand.

Her eyes remained closed and a smile trickled into her features.

Paul squeezed her wrist and gave a light tug.

Sandra's eyes flew open, turning toward Paul. And then she was vertical and splashing. "It's you. I was…"

"Scaring the hell out of me is what you were doing? Are you okay?" He gasped for breath, struggling to speak. "Do you understand how far you are from shore?"

Sandra squinted toward the beach. "Oh. Wow. I just…"

"It doesn't matter. Let's get us both back to shore before the current carries us out farther than I can swim." Paul was tired and hoped Sandra could get herself to the beach unassisted. "Are you a good swimmer?"

"Yes. I'm fine. I think I'll be…"

She seemed confused, surprised by where she was. Or perhaps by being found and brought back from where she'd planned to go.

———

The sound of Rufus barking rose above the sound of the waves. Paul stopped swimming and treaded water, glancing around for Sandra who was not far behind, still performing the front crawl like an Olympic champ. He'd had concerns about her state of mind and ability to make it to shore unaided, but she'd needed no help from him. She'd lagged at first but, a few minutes on, started cycling from breaststroke to front crawl and back again.

When his feet brushed the sandy bottom, Paul dragged his body a few strides before landing on all fours in the now shallow water, Rufus continuing to bark at the water's edge. Paul's ragged breath came in gasps and his arms were leaden. Semi-regular swimming had not prepared him for that kind of distance. He should have grabbed a life preserver before heading into the water.

Hindsight.

But he'd made it. And so had she.

Sandra was on her feet now, hurrying toward Rufus, her legs pushing through the waves. Suddenly unafraid, the little dog leapt into the water, paddling toward her, and she scooped him out of the surf. His bright pink tongue licked her chin, her cheeks, her eyelids, and she began to cry, dropping to the sand when she reached the beach. She cradled Rufus in her arms, face buried in his fur and shoulders shaking.

Paul stood a few feet away, working to catch his breath, unsure of what to do. He didn't know her well enough to insert himself in the moment, and yet wasn't willing to leave her alone. He sat down, arms resting on his knees, chest still heaving, and waited.

He didn't know how long they remained that way, Sandra sobbing into Rufus and he sitting nearby. But, at last, she lifted her head, swiped at her eyes with a now-dry palm, and stared out at the Sea of Cortez.

"I'm sorry I scared you," she said.

"I'm just glad you're all right."

Only the sound of the gulls and surf broke the silence.

"I was floating. I've always liked to float and look up at the sky. There was this cloud that looked like a dolphin, then a boat. And I could feel the current, gentle and warm. I was awake but somehow not awake because … I had this dream …"

She continued to gaze out at the water.

Paul longed to ask the question knocking around in his head, but was at a loss for the words. Had she meant to kill herself?

As if she'd read his mind she said, "I know what you must think." She looked at him then, green eyes reddened by the salt water and tears. "And I'm not suicidal."

The words came without conviction.

Her gaze returned to the rhythm of the sea, her hand stroking Rufus's wet fur. "It's just been a rough couple days and, out there, it felt like all the weight lifted into the sky. I was floating. Just floating and free."

"But you were drifting out to sea. If I hadn't been looking for you, hadn't spotted the little sentinel here, I'm not sure you would have made it back to shore. Sandra…" Her head turned his way, but her eyes didn't meet his. "My guests are welcome to experience Baja in their own way, but I draw the line at sailing off into the Pacific, without a boat."

She sniffed and a smile teased her lips. Reaching out a hand, she lay it on top of Paul's. "And I apologize for nearly crossing that line. Thank you for bringing me back." She gave a light squeeze before returning her hand to Rufus.

"Can I ask what's been so difficult you wished to float off to the horizon?"

Sandra looked to where the sun was making its way toward the sea before standing and setting Rufus on the sand. "This little guy needs his dinner. He's a real stickler when it comes to mealtime. And shouldn't you be whipping up some kind of gourmet fare in the kitchen about now?"

Paul stood and brushed the sand from his boxers, suddenly conscious of wearing only his underpants. "Indeed." He grabbed his clothing from the pile they'd made on the beach, holding the bundle in front of him. "Will you be joining us at Pablo's to-night? The special is Baja-style fish tacos with Carmelita's amazing mango salsa. Not to be missed, and much nicer if it hasn't travelled to your room in a box. The tortillas get soggy from the—if I do say so myself—delicious cabbage slaw. And, the—"

"Okay. Point taken. I will come to Pablo's for dinner. I promise."

"Excellent." He may not get this woman talking, but he could lure her from her room. And, when the need arose, save her life.

Fourteen

Pescadero Palms, Baja California Sur, Mexico

Paul stepped back from the railing he'd been working on. It was no longer crooked or unstable. The patio on the south side of Pescadero Palms was used for sunbathing, but the sun lovers had gone into San Leandro or La Paz for dinner by this hour of the afternoon. Crouching to put things back in the toolbox, he heard the slap of flip-flops approaching.

"Looking good, Pablo." Rod was behind him.

"And less liable to kill someone who leans over for a better view."

"Well, there's that, but business owners don't like to say the word out loud …" he continued in a whisper, "liable."

Paul chuckled. He closed and latched the toolbox and stood to face Rod. "Understood, Captain. Beverage time?"

"Already chilling in the bag. And Melinda sent along some snacks. Are you hungry?"

"That was thoughtful. I am hungry. Lunch was negligible and long ago."

"Great. Get yourself cleaned up and come on down."

When Rod had gone, Paul took one last look at the patio he'd transformed in the past week. The white deck chairs freshly painted, the broken tiles now replaced, flowering vines beaten back to the perimeter, and now the railing sparkled bright blue and would support the weight of a leaning hotel guest.

Pescadero Palms was feeling more and more like home. Having a reason to get up each morning, a purpose to his days, was so gratifying.

Paul changed out of his work clothes and met Rod on the beach. Rod was always seated and halfway through a beer by the time Paul arrived.

"Living the life," Paul said as he sat down.

"Don't I know it." He handed Paul an open Dos Equis. "To the good life."

"Cheers." Paul touched his bottle to Rod's. "This could become a habit."

Rod snorted. "I think it already has."

They sat in silence for a time, observing the darkening sea, the fading sky.

"But I'm almost finished with the work you had in mind, aren't I?" Paul asked.

Rod nodded. "Afraid so, Pablo. You work too hard. I expanded the list early on, but I'm still running out of things for you to do."

"Right. Well, I knew the day would come. Six weeks has been a good run. I didn't expect it to last this long."

"I'd expected the work to take longer, frankly, but I was basing it on my speed as a man with twenty years on you … who is easily distracted by sitting on the beach or going fishing."

Paul laughed.

"You're a hard worker, and a pleasure to have around. Thanks for all you've done." Rod lifted his beer in a salute.

"No. Thank *you*. A seaside home for six weeks free of charge has been a welcome respite." Paul looked down the green neck of his bottle at the liquid below. "Not to mention the daily beverages."

"You're welcome to stay another week or so, and I'll give you a reference if you want to seek other work in the area. You've got quite the array of skills."

"And you've not even tasted my cooking."

"He cooks too? Why doesn't that surprise me?"

"Not that any of it did my marriage much good." During a previous beer-on-the-beach session, Paul shared the full story of his marriage and its bitter end.

"Perhaps you're destined for a different life and it took a major kick in the ass to get you moving."

"I would have preferred a strongly-worded letter."

"You Brits." Rod was smiling out at the sea.

"Thanks for the offer of a recommendation, but, as much as I'd love to, I don't expect to stay in Mexico. Despite translating my name to Pablo, we both know it's not legal for me to work here. And I don't possess the resources to retire. I'll likely head back to England. I've been on the road for eight months and, at some point, I do need to go home."

"Do you?"

"What else?"

"You could buy the hotel from me." Rod was still staring out at the water.

"Buy The Palms? How many beers have you had, old man?"

Rod turned his gaze to Paul then, his eyes clear and bright. "Just this one and I'm serious. You're perfect for the Pescadero Palms and it for you. Watching you work these past weeks has shown me I've aged beyond this place's needs. It requires the injection of some youth, some energy. Melinda wants to be closer to the grandkids, she'd like me to play more golf, but I can't let this place go to just anyone. It's not like my hardware stores. And you're not just anyone, Pablo."

"I'm not sure I'd call forty-four youthful. And, I may have energy, but not money."

"Didn't you say your ex-wife would be generous with the proceeds from your condo?"

"Well, yes, but by the time I repay my mate for eight months of travelling most of it will be spent."

"Which brings me to my second idea. Your movie-star friend. Maybe he'd like to invest?"

"In a Mexican beach property? I doubt that. He's not really a tropics kind of guy."

"Even if it was *your* Mexican beach property? From what you've said, he's as good a friend as a guy could have, and finances aren't much of an obstacle. But, never mind all that. Aside from the money, which we can sort, does the idea have appeal? Can you see yourself as the owner of my beloved Palms?"

Paul looked over his shoulder at the hotel, its fresh coat of white paint glowing peach in the evening light, its walls rising out of the desert surroundings. Owner of a Mexican beach hotel. That wasn't something on his bucket list. But then maybe he had a new bucket.

Paul called Mark the day after his talk with Rod, asked him if he'd like to come for a visit, told him he'd discovered a great Mexican retreat. He didn't mention his desire to *buy* the Mexican retreat.

Much to Paul's surprise, his friend agreed to come, with enthusiasm. He'd said, "I'm between films at the moment and Serena is driving me mad so Mexico sounds ideal. Put a half dozen cervezas in the fridge and I'll be on the first flight out."

Three days later, Paul waited in the La Paz airport for Mark's arrival. He wiped his wet palms on the back of his shorts. Travel funds were one thing, loaning money to buy real estate, Mexican real estate, was a much different deal. They'd always supported each other, and Paul had been there for Mark many times in all kinds of ways, but this would be a huge ask. He'd considered making his proposal over the phone but knew Pescadero Palms would be a better sell in person. The charm of the Mediterranean-style architecture, the sea right on its doorstep, and the entire place looking fresh as a result of Paul's weeks of work.

He'd been early, not wanting Mark to have to wait in the airport after fifteen hours of travel, and now the flight from Mexico City was late. Paul's gaze followed the AeroMexico plane as it touched down and began its taxi to the terminal.

He had a plan A and B prepared depending on Mark's state when he arrived. Having flown all night, he might be fatigued and ready to retire to the hotel, but it was now afternoon in the UK so it could also be cocktail hour. Although still morning in Baja, Paul was certain they could locate a beer or a drink along the Malecon in La Paz.

The plane rolled to a stop in front of the concourse and safety-vested staff went to work chocking wheels, setting up pylons, and driving out baggage carriers. Paul assumed Mark had travelled first class so would be one of the first to disembark. He wiped his hands on his shorts again. He was being ridiculous. Mark was his oldest friend, and even if unwilling or unable to invest in Paul's crazy idea, they'd have a good visit.

When the stairs were in place, passengers began to file out through the open door. A man in a business suit exited first, followed by a woman and a young child, and then Mark. Paul's friend stopped at the top of the stairs and pulled his sunglasses down onto the bridge of his nose. Ever the film star. Paul smiled. Despite the passage of many years, it still struck him as odd that this man he'd known since childhood was now one of the best-known actors in the UK.

Mark had succeeded where Paul had not, simple as that. But he harboured no bitterness. Mark deserved the success he'd achieved. He was talented, good looking and, so he claimed, rather lucky. Paul considered himself average in the looks department, a bit too white bread for the interesting character roles, and not attractive enough for a leading man. He'd worked hard to learn the craft of acting, while Mark's ability came naturally, as though born to it. Was Paul born to run a small hotel in Baja?

The first of the passengers reached the terminal and disappeared inside the secured area.

Being in an airport reminded Paul of his first journey out of the UK many months before. How ruined he'd felt, how broken. And now a light had appeared at the end of the great tunnel he'd been travelling through, a tunnel with no discernible destination until now.

The doors slipped open and there was Mark amid a small herd of passengers, sunglasses now perched in his wavy brown hair, a loose cotton shirt over khaki trousers, eyes scanning the waiting crowd. His face lifted in a broad smile when he spotted Paul. "Hutchings!" he called, making his way through the throng of waiting friends and family.

Mark embraced his friend with his free arm, the other toted a shoulder bag and carry-on-sized suitcase.

"Welcome to Mexico," Paul said. "It's great to see you."

Mark stepped back, one hand resting on Paul's shoulder. "You're looking well. You've lost the pasty Englishman thing."

"Thanks, I think. Do you have checked luggage?"

"No. This is it. I scanned the Baja forecast and packed accordingly. It's been raining for days in London. I am looking forward to a week of sunshine."

"A week. That's terrific. I'll show you the sights."

"Right now, the only sight I'm interested in is that of a cold beer in my hand."

"You know it's nine o'clock in the morning here?"

"So they said as we were coming in for a landing but, as the song says, it's five o'clock somewhere—" Mark checked his wristwatch. "At the moment, London."

Fifteen

It was early morning and Paul was behind the front desk at Casa del Mar Azul, balancing receipts from the previous evening in Pablo's. Paperwork was not his favourite part of operating a business, but he liked to monitor the finances and there was no better way. He'd recently taught Elena to balance her portion of the evening, which had shortened the process without removing his eyes from the ball.

Claws clicking on ceramic tile signalled the arrival of Rufus. The dog skittered around behind the desk and propped his front paws against Paul's knee, tail wagging.

"Hey, little dude. What are you doing running around on your own?" When he knelt to give the dog a rub, Rufus flopped down and rolled onto his back, exposing his belly.

"Rufus!" Sandra called from the parking area in front of the hotel. "Rufus, you little bugger. Come!"

The dog offered no sign he'd heard her calling. Paul chuckled. "Should I tell her you're here or are you hiding? Not sure I want to land in trouble on your account." Paul rose and called to the open doorway, "Sandra, he's in here."

She appeared in the bougainvillea-covered archway, looking flustered. "I'm so sorry. He disappeared on me just as we finished our walk." Her eyes roamed the lobby. "Rufus," she said in a deepened tone.

The little dog crept from behind the reception desk, head lowered and tail wagging stiffly between his rear legs.

"You should be sorry," Sandra said. "You scared me." She crouched down and took Rufus's head between her hands, rubbed his ears, and gave him a kiss on top of the nose. "I heard coyotes last night, and they sounded close."

"They normally stay to the hills, but it's a good idea to keep this guy in sight. He's rather snack-sized."

"You hear that, Ruf, snack-sized. Let that be a warning." She gave his head one last rub and stood.

Sandra's eyes were bright this morning. And green. Had they changed colour in the days since she'd arrived? He could have sworn they were a shade of grey.

"You're out and about early this morning. Will you be joining us on the breakfast patio?"

"That is tempting, but I'm off to the market in San Leandro and Ian suggested a tamale place for breakfast."

"Ah, you're meeting Ian. That's good. He seems a decent chap."

The phone rang and Paul went to the desk. "Casa del Mar Azul, good morning." He answered the caller's questions about the hotel and directed the woman to his website if she decided to make a reservation. Sandra was wandering the small lobby, inspecting the paintings on the walls.

When Paul finished with the call, Sandra said, "You have some wonderful pieces. Are these by local artists?"

"This one is," Paul gestured to a still life of a grouping of Mexican pottery, "but the others are by an art-teacher friend of mine and her students."

Sandra was looking at an oil painting of San Leandro, its coloured buildings stacked on the hillside. "Is this one hers?"

"Yes, that is one of Jenna's. As is the beach scene down the hall and," he pointed to a desert landscape near the entrance, "that one, my favourite."

"They're beautiful. I love her use of light and the brush strokes, like here," she pointed, "are so unique."

"Spoken like an artist. Do you paint?"

"I do. Acrylics, mostly. Some oil and I've dabbled in watercolour."

Sandra moved on to another piece and studied it. "And this was painted by one of her students? But not someone local?"

"Correct on both counts. Jenna is an old friend who teaches art back in the UK. She brings a group here once a year on a painting holiday."

"Well, she's very good, and obviously an excellent instructor if these others are all by her students." Paintings lined the hallway to the rooms.

"She is talented, yes, and smart and beautiful and …"

Sandra's eyebrows lifted in a question.

"… and married," Paul finished.

"Oh. Too bad. The one who got away?" A smile transformed her entire face. She'd looked so much older when she'd first stepped from her SUV, but now Paul guessed her to be closer to forty than fifty.

"Something like that." Paul glanced down at his flip-flops, noticing the woven band on the left foot was unraveling. "And then I creeped her on the internet not long after I moved here and got in touch via her website." His eyes went to Jenna's desert scene he loved. He'd been so surprised at the welcome response he'd received to his initial email, as if they were just old friends who'd lost touch. In addition to all of her other qualities, Jenna was forgiving. "She told me how much she'd been dying to offer painting retreats, I told her about Mar Azul, and now she comes with a group every year." Paul sighed, realizing too late it was audible to Sandra. "But, anyway, if you'd like to paint while staying here, she keeps some easels and supplies in storage. You're welcome to them."

"Thanks. I'll think about that. Not sure there's time. I should be … thinking about … going home." Her eyes darted to the clock above the reception desk. "Right now I should be going to the village. I'm walking. Ian's offered to give me a ride back with any market finds. Is there anything I can pick up for you?"

"I could use some lemons if they're nice. And, since you've got a ride, the biggest bag they have."

"Done." Sandra turned to leave. "Rufus, come on." The dog was lying with his head on Paul's foot.

"Are you taking him with you?"

"No. He's not always great with other dogs, larger dogs in particular, and Ian mentioned there are a few roaming the streets and the market. I'll leave him in my room. Rufus, let's go. I know you're not deaf."

The wiry dog remained where he was. "You can leave him with me if you like. He can be my sidekick this morning."

"Won't you be in the kitchen?"

"Yes, but it's my kitchen and if he stays off the countertops and the food stays off the floor, we should be fine. People worry too much about dogs near food preparation."

"He's a real kitchen dog, so he'd love that. But, if he gets in the way or isn't staying where he's supposed to, please put him in my room." She knelt down and stroked the dog's head. "You. Be. Good. Hear me? Stay."

Rufus's whiskery brows followed Sandra as she disappeared beyond the bougainvillea, but he didn't move from his resting place. Paul looked down at him, wishing the little dog could fill him in on which one of life's tragedies had befallen his mistress. Lost love? Betrayal? Death? Rufus stared up at Paul, his brown eyes giving nothing away. "Can't talk or sworn to secrecy? Well, I needn't know as long as you agree to sound the alarm if she gets in trouble again. I had a lifeline tossed to me when I was in over my head, so I'll be there to throw one to her. Deal?"

Rufus jumped to his feet and wagged his tail.

Sixteen

Two days into Mark's stay, Paul hadn't yet sprung his proposal on his friend. He was waiting for the perfect opportunity and it hadn't presented itself. Mark was still in his room and Paul was sitting on the rooftop patio, watching the sun rise from the Sea of Cortez. Would he tire of this view, this place? Not possible.

"Here you are." Rod was climbing the last few stairs to the patio. "Beautiful morning." He dragged a chair up beside Paul's.

"You're here early," Paul said. Rod typically wandered in around ten.

"I wanted to catch you alone. Melinda keeps asking and so I must inquire, have you talked to your friend yet?"

"No. I'm sorry. He's been working through jet lag and has some stuff going on with his marriage. I don't want to add to his troubles."

"Add to whose troubles?"

Paul spun in his chair to find Mark standing at the top of the stairs. "Mark. Hey. We were just enjoying the sunrise. Come join us."

"And talking about me?"

Rod stood. "Well, there are some guests wanting to go fishing today so I should run home, get myself organized. Take my chair." He gestured to the wooden deck chair, bright white thanks to Paul's paintbrush.

Mark looked from Paul to Rod. "I get the feeling I've missed something."

"Have a seat. I'll explain," Paul said.

Once Rod left, Mark sat down next to Paul. "So, are you and Rod having an affair? Is that what I've stumbled upon?" He was doing his best to appear serious, but the corners of his mouth couldn't keep from curving upward.

"Yes, that's it. You had to know sometime. There is … someone else."

Mark lay the back of a hand on his forehead as if in a swoon. "*I am one who loved not wisely but too well.*" He leaned toward Paul, close enough for Paul to smell his friend's aftershave, something masculine and expensive. "And when I flew all this way to see you."

"I wished to tell you in person. It seemed the decent thing."

"Okay, Hutchings, enough theatrics. I'm guessing you were speaking of *my* troubles. Just what is it you don't want to add to them?"

Paul studied his friend of thirty-plus years, those kind, brown eyes locked on his own. *Just say the words, Paul.* "Okay. I invited you here to make a proposal, or more of an appeal for an enormous favour."

"And I thought you just missed me."

"Well, that too. I wanted to see you, for you to see this place. Do you like it, The Palms?"

"Yes, of course. What's not to like? And Rod seems a good fellow."

Paul and Rod's late afternoon beer on the beach had become a trio since Mark's arrival.

"He is. And a rather old fellow, who wants to retire, as does his wife. You'll meet Melinda tonight at dinner."

"And …?"

"And he's offered to sell me the Pescadero Palms."

Mark stared at him, eyes now swimming with questions. "Ri-i-ight … and you're interested in being a hotelier? In Mexico?"

"I am."

"I realize your life has been upended but, Paul, this is an enormous change. Are you certain it's the best time to be making major life decisions? What about your career?"

"If you're referring to acting, my career doesn't exist. It's never fully supported me, and I don't expect it will start anytime soon. In fact, things seem to be going in the opposite direction. I'm finished with acting. It hasn't worked out for me like it has for you."

"But it's your passion. I wouldn't even be an actor if you hadn't led the way. I owe every success I've had to you."

"And I'm thrilled to have been part of your success, but it didn't happen for me. The film industry and Rachel have made it abundantly clear it's time for me to move on. I want to move on to *this*." Paul swept his arm from the sea to the hills behind the hotel. "Since the life I lived in the UK ended eight months ago, I've spent my time doing some soul searching. The search brought me here, to Rod and his Pescadero Palms. When it came time to think about moving on to what's next, I didn't want to go. I feel like I've come home, discovered some part of myself, some whole person I didn't know existed."

"Pablo?" Mark had found amusement in Rod's nickname for his friend.

Paul laughed. "Yes, perhaps Pablo. I've always wanted a house, you know, a big house with a garden, and I've lived in a flat my entire life."

"But you'd have to share *your house* with twenty or thirty strangers." Mark mocked a shudder, his shoulders twitching.

"But I like that part. I've been helping with the hosting duties and I've loved it and the guests seek me out. A few of them assumed I *was* the owner."

"Well, if you're certain, I'm behind you, happy for you."

This is my opening. Paul wrung his hands together in his lap. "The thing is," he took a deep breath, "I can't do it on my own. The money from the divorce will cover what I borrowed from you for travelling but—"

Mark held up a hand like a traffic cop. "That wasn't a loan. Think of it as repayment for all you've done for me over the years. If not for you—well, we need not get into that long list. You use the settlement in whatever way moves your life along a chosen path."

"Thanks, that's generous." Paul looked down at his clenched hands. "But on the heels of that generosity, I need to ask for something more."

Mark leaned back in his chair. "Okay. I'm listening."

Just say the words. "I need a loan, a rather substantial one, to buy The Palms. I'm not in any position to borrow through standard channels. I'm willing to contribute every penny of the divorce settlement as a down payment, but that's as much as I'm able to do."

Paul scrutinized his friend's face, trying to read his reaction. He realized he had no idea if Mark even had access to the kind of money needed to buy the hotel. He lived extravagantly, owned two homes, and always had a pair of new cars. Paul assumed he had a fat bank account based on the recent level of his salaries, but maybe he spent to the level of his earnings. Maybe Paul had just jeopardized a valued friendship by even asking. The longer Mark remained silent, the more the thoughts clawed through Paul's mind. He hadn't even told him an amount. "The loan—"

"Of course. Of course I'll help you. If you're sure it's what you want, if this is your passion, your new life. I'd rather loan it to you than watch Serena spend it all on trinkets and glamour. What kind of money are we talking about?"

Paul pulled a folded sheet of paper from a back pocket and laid out his full plan for Mark. The purchase price, the interest rate, the revenue and expenses, the amount he could afford in monthly payments.

Mark pointed to the number at the bottom of the page. "There's not enough left for you."

"I won't need much. I'll live in the hotel. Other than food, my living expenses are all included in here." He gestured to the expense section of his handwritten budget.

"Meaning you'll be stranded here."

"I don't see it that way. Before you and I went to Australia, I'd never left the UK. I'm quite content to stay in one place, especially now that I've had my grand adventure."

"All right. But there is one other issue with these calculations."

Mark was holding the sheet of paper and Paul leaned over to look. What had he missed?

Pointing to the *interest on loan* item, Mark said, "I'm disappointed with this rate—."

"I know it's low. I wrestled with the number, but it's the best I can do, at least in the beginning. I have ideas for future revenue streams. We could increase the rate in a year or two."

Mark cleared his throat. "I'm disappointed you think I'd charge you interest. How long have we been friends, Hutchings? If you hadn't dragged me off to LAMDA, I wouldn't have access to this kind of money, ever. There'll be a loan but I won't accept interest."

"Now that I can't do, give you nothing in return."

"Then give me a room when I come to visit."

"You'll visit?"

"I'll have to. From what I see here," he shook the paper, "you'll be chained to this place for life so, if I want to see my oldest friend, I'll have no choice. Besides, I rather like the view." His eyes shifted eastward and he squinted into the sunrise.

Paul felt the burn of tears and blinked. "I don't know what to say."

Mark extended a hand. "Just shake my hand and say it's a deal. Before I decide I'm not willing to be party to your plan of moving to another continent."

Seventeen

Baja California Sur, Mexico

Dinner with Rod and Melinda was a celebratory event once Paul shared the news of the sale. Melinda's face, when he informed them he'd secured the loan to buy the hotel, was nothing short of illuminated.

Their adobe-style home overlooked the sea from its hillside location, and the four of them sat outside on the terrace.

"I love Pescadero Palms, and Mexico, and I've enjoyed living by the sea, but I want to be closer to family," Melinda said. "The grandchildren are growing up and, in no time, they'll not be interested in spending time with Gran and Gramps. And, exciting news, Wendy is pregnant, so she and Wayne are also ready to return home."

"You're headed back to Michigan then?" Paul asked.

"Lord, no," Rod said. "After eight years in this climate we wouldn't survive a single winter."

"Our kids are scattered across the country, so our options are open. We're planning to settle in Albuquerque." Melinda reached over and took her husband's hand. "Rod's not keen to leave *old* Mexico, so New Mexico seems like a compromise."

"And my lovely wife has agreed to a motorhome, for ease of travel to our various children's locations."

Melinda sighed. "Yes, I have. Although I'd prefer to fly."

"I would have said the same thing a year ago," Paul said, "but travelling by road through North America was the experience of a lifetime. A motorhome is a terrific way to go." Rod winked at him in thanks. "By the way, I didn't reach New Mexico, so I may have to pay you two a visit at some point."

"And you'd be most welcome," Melinda said. "You too," she said to Mark. Despite initially being star-struck, Melinda had treated Mark like family after the first half hour of their visit, and he'd responded in kind, never the aloof celebrity. "After years of having fifteen rooms available to host visitors, we plan to have at least two guest rooms in our new home."

"When do you plan to leave?" Mark asked.

"Just as soon as the paperwork is complete," Melinda said. "We'll fly to Albuquerque to shop for a house and come back for our things. This place is a rental so it's just a matter of giving notice to the landlord."

Rod was not as exuberant as Melinda about the topic of conversation, their leaving Baja. He listened and sipped on his beer, nodding here and there, abnormally quiet. Paul used a lull in the discussion to divert things in his direction. "So, Rod, tell me more about this motorhome you're proposing to buy." And he was off, sharing his research on diesel versus gasoline, layout options, sizes, and weights. The completion of so much research on future hometowns and modes of travel suggested Rod and Melinda had been confident he would purchase the hotel.

Paul had been less assured and, with fewer than twelve hours to let it sink in, the whole thing was still feeling surreal. He, Paul Hutchings, failed actor and jilted husband, would be a Mexican hotelier or, in the language of his new homeland, a *hotelero.*

Paul's old SUV bounced down the narrow road leading from Rod and Melinda's hillside home to the main road. Although only a fifteen-minute walk each way from Pescadero Palms, it was largely highway with no shoulder and not a safe place to walk after dark.

"Good job this is a dry climate. This road must turn to a mudslide in the rain," Mark said.

"It does indeed. They slept at The Palms one night after a monsoon-type event, weren't sure they'd make it home."

"Your friend Rod doesn't seem pleased about this arrangement, other than the motorhome. I feel complicit in pulling the rug of life out from under him."

"It would happen with or without your involvement, not for me, perhaps, but for another buyer. He's been holding out for the *right* person about as long as Melinda will allow. She's finished with this place."

"I know how that feels."

"What are you finished with?"

"Oh, not me, my wife. I think she's finished with me."

"I'm … sorry. I sensed things weren't great, but I didn't realize …" Paul did his best to sound the concerned friend, but it was difficult given his less-than-friendly relationship with Mark's spouse.

"It's all right. I feel much the same, other than I dislike failing." He paused. "She's been staying with a *friend* for about a month. The word *separation* hasn't been spoken, but I expect that's where we're at."

"And this friend?"

"Is a man. Who she tells me is just an old mate giving her a space to get her head on straight." Mark was staring out the side window at the sea passing by in the moonlight. "But I don't believe that for a minute. She's Serena. She doesn't have male friends."

"So your wife just moved in with another bloke?"

"So it seems."

"Blimey. That's shit."

"Hm. And it'll get worse if the media get wind."

"Well, if you need a place to hide, I've just purchased an obscure hotel in an out-of-the-way spot."

Paul turned off the highway and wound down the short drive to The Palms, parking near the entrance.

They climbed out of the vehicle and Mark's gaze turned upward to the sign on the wall of the hotel. "What are you going to call the place?"

"I wasn't planning to change it."

"Oh, Hutchings, you truly must. Pescadero Palms sounds like an old Las Vegas inn with cheap drinks and women to match."

Paul's eyes went to the scrolling writing with a palm tree forming the L. "I thought it was rather catchy."

"As are most hotel names in Las Vegas. You need something classy, something that says boutique hotel."

"Boutique. Is that what I want?"

"Boutique is what tourists with money want so, therefore, it is what you want."

Paul leaned against the grill of the 4Runner and crossed his arms. The white stucco walls of The Palms glowed in the moonlight, the red tile roof and blue trim darkened by the shadows. "Well, since it possesses the look, maybe a Mediterranean-sounding name."

"You're in Mexico. Stay with that." Mark joined him at the front of the 4Runner. "What was it you said about always wanting a house? How about casa something or other?"

"Casa. I like the homey feel of that, and the Spanish. I know. How about … Casa Pablo!" Paul threw an arm toward the hotel.

"Fun but, no. Something longer, more posh. What struck you first about the place?"

"Location, location, location. The azure blue of Cortez right on the doorstep."

"Mm. Cortez is a good word." Mark rubbed at his chin and stared at the hotel. "Casa Cortez maybe, or Casa del Cortez, if that's correct in Spanish."

The words rolled around in Paul's mind—house, casa, blue, Cortez, sea. "I don't know the Spanish but, if it rolls off the tongue nicely, how about house of the blue sea, translated to," he gestured to Mark, "your idea, casa something or other."

"Well, I just happen to have a translator in my trouser pocket." Mark pulled out his iPhone and typed into a browser search bar. He hit enter and smiled at what he saw.

"What? What is it?"

Mark handed his phone to Paul. On the screen were the words Casa del Mar Azul.

Eighteen

The small, open-air deck space of the breakfast patio was crowded, all six tables occupied. Paul scanned the diners seated in white wicker chairs. Most were guests of Casa del Mar Azul, but he spotted a few faces he didn't recognize, likely tourists from San Leandro. Up at the front, with the best view, sat Sandra and Ian. Paul smiled. It warmed him to see her mingling in the land of the living.

"Good morning." Both heads turned in his direction as he approached. The remnants of their meal lay scattered across the table. "How was your breakfast?" He set down the bag of oranges he'd pulled from cold storage.

"Everything was delicious," Ian said.

"That Tuscan omelette was … wow. What's in there, besides the obvious?" Sandra asked.

"It's the local eggs that make the difference. I get them from Carmelita's brother. You'll have to ask him what he feeds his chickens."

Ian grinned at Sandra. "I guess you need to stick around if you want to solve the mystery of the delicious eggs."

"Or come back," she responded. Her eyes swung upward to Paul. "I'm leaving today. Your RV friends got in touch and they're headed north, so I am too. Sorry for the short notice."

"Oh. Well …" His friends typically left at the end of April, which was still more than a week away. He'd suggested to Sandra that she caravan with other travellers on her way home and this couple wintered just north of La Paz in their coach. The timing had seemed perfect.

"They said something about an issue with their house in Colorado, an extra heavy snow pack, potential for flooding, fun stuff like that," Sandra said. "And Ian has offered to travel with me to La Paz, even though it's unnecessary."

"I need to go anyway," he said. "There's a bar interested in hiring me and they want to meet in person. And … I need to be sure you get on the right road north."

"Did I mention I drove down here?"

"Well, yes, but that was a while ago."

"Have they changed the route?"

Smiling and even joking. Baja had been good for Sandra, Mar Azul performing its healing as it had for him five years earlier. Was it the climate, the proximity of the water, the hotel itself, or some magical combination of the three? Perhaps it was like the Tuscan omelette, somehow greater than the sum of its parts.

"I appreciate your looking out for me, both of you. You're true gentlemen." She glanced at her wristwatch. "Bernie and Joanne want to be on the road by the *crack of noon* they said, so I need to get loaded and going." Sandra swallowed the last of her coffee and stood. "Will you be in the lobby in about an hour?" she asked Paul.

"I'll be there just as soon as I check on the situation in the kitchen. Carmelita handles most of the morning orders, but it's busy today and the omelettes are my domain. By now, she probably thinks I'm out picking these oranges." He retrieved the bag from the floor.

A woman from a neighbouring table called to Paul, "Excuse me. Can we please get more coffee?"

Paul assured her he would be right back with the pot.

"If you're short-handed, I can pour coffee and clear a few tables before I go to my room. There's time," Sandra said.

"Absolutely not. You're a guest."

"Well, I'm not." Ian started stacking the plates and cups from their table. "And, as a lifelong musician, I have plenty of restaurant experience."

"You check the kitchen," Sandra said, "and we'll refill coffee cups and clear away dishes."

Paul stared at her.

"Go. We know where the coffee station is."

Two more omelettes and another round of coffee refills later, Paul took up his position behind the desk in the lobby. He needed more help. Arturo was proving himself to be quite capable. Maybe he could assist with breakfast, at least on the weekends.

He drew Sandra Lyall's card from its slot. Eighteen days since she'd arrived looking like a stray seeking sanctuary. He wondered again about her story. What would cause a forty-year-old woman to drive twenty-five hundred miles across two borders to a reach a destination she'd never heard of? It was a mystery and would remain so. Anytime he'd asked or attempted to move the conversation in that direction, she'd changed the subject or left the room.

The rumpled brochure she'd produced that first night lay tucked underneath the counter. Pulling it out, he read the front flap aloud. "*Visit Casa del Mar Azul and drink in serenity.*"

Precisely how it felt to him when he'd first arrived, first bought the place, like a much-needed drink after a long thirst. So he'd printed it right there on the cover of the brochure, and his words had drawn Sandra here, and possibly others. On the advice of a marketing consultant, Paul changed his promotional materials and dropped the tag line. He pulled a new brochure from its place in the stand and set it beside its older counterpart. The new one looked more professional, but those alluring words were absent. If they drew in the broken and adrift seeking refuge, they needed to be there. He was almost out of stock and would make the change on the reprint.

Rufus came racing through the front entrance and behind the desk. "Hey little friend. I'm told you're leaving us today. Who will be my sidekick now?"

"You'll just have to get yourself a dog." Sandra walked up to the counter, dropping her shoulder bag on its surface.

"I had a guest serving coffee this morning and you think I have time for a dog?"

Sandra smiled. "I guess not. At least not until you hire some help. What about that nice young man who works in Pablo's in the evening? He's very sweet and quite a charmer."

"But he's also in school for another two years. I can normally juggle things in the mornings. It was the run on omelettes that made this morning tricky."

"Well, that's what happens when you create something so irresistible. Word gets around and more and more people order. I'm coming back next year, just for the Tuscan omelette."

"You're planning to return to us?"

"I am. It's been so … so very …" She looked up at the ceiling as her eyes filled. "Just … thank you." She was smiling now, the tears pushed back. "And I didn't even paint. I understand why your friend brings a group here every year. It's beautiful, so inspiring. I have to come back to paint the Sea of Cortez."

"Well, we can arrange transport from La Paz or Cabo. Just call with your flight times."

"Oh no, I'll drive again. I like to drive. But break it up a little more and—"

"And not travel alone?"

"Right. Yes. And not travel alone, if I can find people headed here at the right time."

"Talk to Bernie and Joanne. They regularly connect with other travellers and know where to find them."

Rufus had returned to the front side of the desk and was lying at Sandra's feet. "And I'll leave Rufus at home, having discovered you don't actually take pets. I saw it written somewhere. You should have told me."

Warmth flooded Paul's face. "Rufus wasn't a problem, for me or any of the guests."

"Well, I appreciate your taking us in, despite our bedraggled appearance and one of us having two too many legs."

"It was my pleasure." He laid Sandra's receipt on the countertop and offered her the old brochure. "Would you like this?"

She took it in her hands, rubbing her thumbs over its smooth surface. "Finding this single piece of paper was like spotting a tiny light at the end of a deep, dark tunnel." Her eyes rose to Paul's face, again the tears welling in her lower lids. "And I arrived to find a remarkable, perfect place, the drink of serenity this promised." She raised the brochure before tucking it into her bag. "You've been a lifesaver, you and your Casa del Mar Azul. Thank you so so much." She placed a hand over her heart. "From the very bottom of this broken heart."

It was the most she'd shared of her sadness, and Paul knew it was all she would say. There was no point in asking questions. Maybe next year she'd be ready to talk.

He moved around the counter and extended a hand. "Until next time then." She placed her hand in his and pulled him into an embrace, hugging him tightly.

When she stepped back, there were wet tracks down her cheeks. She threw her bag over a shoulder and picked up Rufus, planting a kiss on the top of his nose. "Time to go home, buddy."

Paul watched Sandra pass through the archway lined with bougainvillea, her long skirt swaying, Rufus peeking back over her shoulder. He would love to take credit for being the light at the end of her tunnel, but he knew the magic belonged to Casa del Mar Azul, the house of the blue sea.

A Note from the Author

Dear Reader,

Thank you for reading **Becoming Pablo**. If you enjoyed the story, a review on Goodreads, Amazon, Kobo, or any other book-lover hangout online, would be much appreciated. Indie authors rely on this word-of-mouth method of reaching out to readers.

If you'd like to know what happens next in the lives of Paul, Sandra, Mark, and Ian, **House of the Blue Sea** is available in print or ebook at all major book retailers. Visit my website at **teresavanbryce.com** for a complete list.

And, while you're on my website, sign up to receive offers of **free books** and updates on what I'm writing.

In the meantime, turn the page for the prologue and first chapters of **House of the Blue Sea**...

About the Author

Teresa van Bryce lives on twenty acres of prairie in Alberta, Canada, escaping to somewhere south of that when the snow flies. She was published in a number of equine magazines before turning her pen to her true literary love ... fiction. When Teresa isn't writing, she's sailing alongside her husband, walking with her  dog, riding one of her three horses, or off exploring the natural world with trailer in tow. Visit her online at teresavanbryce.com, or follow her on Facebook, Instagram, or Twitter.

House of the *Blue Sea*

Teresa van Bryce

Prologue

The road, like two dark ribbons on a sheet of bright, white paper, merged into blackness beyond the reach of her headlights. Sandra blinked, then blinked again, squeezing her eyes tight before opening them. Even though she was travelling at just sixty kilometres an hour, the falling snow seemed to drive directly into her eyes, hypnotic and disorienting. She rolled down the car window, the rush of cold air scentless and sharp—but the blast of winter air wasn't working. She was going to have to stop. Probably best not to cross the Canada/US border this late at night anyway. There wasn't much for miles on the other side but wide open Montana cattle country.

It felt like a week since she'd woken up at home this morning and looked out at the coming dawn, the grey light crawling in through the slats of the bedroom blind. It was snowing, and she'd burrowed further down under the covers, pulling them up over her head to block out the light. Rufus whined from his bed on the floor beside hers and she lifted the blanket, patting the mattress to invite him under the covers with her. When the little dog had settled into the curve of her body, they'd both fallen asleep, feeling each other's heartbeats, his wiry coat pressed against her flannel pajamas.

It was nearly noon by the time Sandra dragged herself from the warmth of her bed and headed downstairs to make coffee. Rufus trotted beside, undoubtedly hoping for breakfast, looking up at her with each step. When her bare feet touched the cool of the main floor hardwood she stopped. The cordless phone lay on its back, alone in the middle of the dining room table, noiselessly shouting the many messages it held. She turned and took the first two stairs before stopping again, her hand resting on the railing. Frozen. She stood. And then, just like that, she knew … she needed to get away. She couldn't take one more phone call, one more card, one more well-meaning friend unable to carry on a normal conversation.

Despite the sense of urgency that grew in her as the afternoon wore on, Sandra cleaned the house as she always did before going on a trip—a habit left over from growing up with her mother. If there'd been a fire in the middle of the night her mother would have had to make the bed before escaping the blaze. Sandra filled a duffel bag with a few random items of clothing and toiletries, put Rufus in the car, and set off south on the Queen Elizabeth II Highway.

That was hours ago. The weather was making it slow going, particularly after dark. She still didn't know where she was going, only that she had to go. South. In four hours that was all she'd come up with. South. Out of the cold, out of winter and away from this interminable heaviness.

One

It was like following a house. *On the road … still — Marion and Tom Braithwaite* was written in scrolling purple font across the back of the motorhome. Below the lettering, a multi-coloured graphic of a map of the US had all but a few of the states filled in to show the places they had travelled. Barney. They called their RV Barney. It was grey but with a slight lilac hue, which is why, Sandra assumed, it had been given the name.

How different she felt from four years ago when she'd travelled this same road. When she thought back to that trip it seemed she'd driven the entire way in darkness, but of course that wasn't the case. She'd left home at night in a blinding snow but travelled the rest of the distance in daylight. Darkness had been a state of mind.

She had met the Braithwaites her second trip south. They

were on a blog of Baja-bound travellers looking to caravan up for the journey. It was safer that way—of course it was. With a more sane mind, it was clearly a good idea. When she'd first met Marion and Tom they'd chastised her for the reckless behaviour the year before. Sandra was younger than their sixty years by just a decade, but they took her under their wing like a daughter and spoke to her as such.

Almost at the border, a few more miles and they'd be in Mexico, and in those few feet across an invisible line on the earth, everything changed. From Canada to the US was barely noticeable but going into Mexico you instantly knew you had crossed a border. The flat storefronts with bold lettering painted on their faces for signs, small late model cars and trucks replacing the herds of SUVs further north, old school buses used for urban transit, and a general increase in activity and noise that couldn't be attributed to any one thing. Food and music were everywhere. Just try to walk one block in a Mexican town without finding something to eat or hearing music piped out onto the street from a restaurant or store. It was like an assault on the senses, but in a good way. Sandra loved it.

From the Mexican border to the south end of the Baja Peninsula required about twenty hours of driving. They'd done it in two days that first year, she and Rufus, pulling off the road before it got dark; at least she'd had that much sense. She had been looking forward to this year's journey since the first snowflake hit the ground back home, and this time she would stay longer. Life at home wasn't exactly hectic, now that she was more of an arm's length owner in the company without a daily role, but friends, family, animals, and a house offered their own kind of pressure, one that Sandra enjoyed being free of during her Mexico stays. She hadn't brought Rufus along since that first unplanned journey south and, although she missed his constant presence in her day, she revelled in the freedom of daily life in Baja, like she was an observer, dipping in and out of the world as and when she chose, not beholden to anyone or anything.

Four years ago, she wouldn't have thought it possible to feel happy being alone, now it was the key to her contentedness. Each winter she felt more at home, more at peace, the beauty and tranquility of the Sea of Cortez filling the void that had threatened to swallow her each day that first year. She'd drifted through those days in a fog that was finally burned away by the Mexican sunshine in the final week of the visit.

And now Baja drew her like Mecca, its desert landscape and turquoise blue waters pulling at her each winter and inspiring the work she'd begun on canvas her second trip down. It was such an easy place to be inspired, and oh-so-easy to get caught up in the pace of life in Mexico—*mañana.*

Sandra took a deep breath as she climbed out of her SUV; the moist air carried the mingled scents of salt, seaweed and something floral. She stretched her arms above her head and turned slowly in place, taking in the 360-degree view. A small boutique hotel, Casa del Mar Azul rested seaside, its white-washed face looking onto the Sea of Cortez; its backdrop the foothills of the Sierra de la Laguna mountain range. Casa del Mar Azul—House of the Blue Sea.

Mar Azul reminded Sandra of photos she'd seen of Spanish seaside villas. In fact, it was what had drawn her here in the first place. Four years before, on her second night in Mexico, she'd stopped at a small hotel and a brochure in their lobby caught her attention. It had an image of a white and blue villa, sitting right at the edge of the sea. Ever since she'd written a report on the Mediterranean in junior high, Sandra had wanted to visit Spain, but when she swore off flying in her early twenties, she gave up the idea of travel to Europe, unless she wanted to drive across North America and take a boat over the Atlantic. *Visit Casa del Mar Azul and drink in serenity* was written below the photo. It had called to her four years ago, and every year since.

Sandra leaned into the car and adjusted the rear view mirror so she could see herself. The humidity was playing havoc with her straw-coloured hair so she tucked it behind her ears in an attempt to tame the curls and waves. The hours on the road had painted faint shadows under her green eyes, but the heat had given her high cheekbones a natural blush so, all-in-all, she looked presentable.

She pulled her purse and a leather shoulder bag from the passenger seat and took the pebbled pathway to the hotel entrance, the tiny white stones crunching under her canvas deck shoes. The bougainvillea hung thick and fragrant from the roof's overhang, and its bright pink blossoms brushed Sandra's shoulder as she passed. She stopped and leaned her face toward a cluster of flowers and inhaled their honeysuckle-like scent. She closed her eyes, the feel of the air surrounding her like loving arms.

"Ms. Lyall, so good to see you again. Welcome back." Paul was standing in the doorway to the lobby, watching her.

Sandra took the final steps to the hotel, reaching for his outstretched hand. "And it is very good to be back. I've been looking forward to visiting Mar Azul since … well, since I left last year. I was just enjoying the captivating aromas of Cortez."

"Ah yes." He tilted his head back and inhaled. "It's easy to become complacent. Thanks for the reminder. Come in, come in." Paul led her inside and took up his station behind the front desk.

There was something about Paul's face that said *welcome* even before he spoke the word; and the lobby of Casa del Mar Azul reflected his warm nature. Two overstuffed chairs sat along one wall with a rattan table between them covered in magazines, while the walls were decorated with art and keepsakes from Paul's life and travels.

Sandra gestured to the open windows along the side of the lobby. "The weather is perfect, as always."

"I order it up special for your visits. No rain, no storms off the Pacific, and enough wind to keep you cool."

"Well, thank you. This northerner appreciates the refreshing breeze."

Paul Hutchings was an ex-pat from England and his face showed the telltale signs of fifty-plus years of smiling. Sandra's first exposure to British culture had been through her older brother William's passion for everything Monty Python, and Paul reminded her of one of the Python actors, the fair-haired one with the incredibly happy face. (Although Paul's fair hair appeared to be exiting stage left.) When she'd first met him four years earlier, she'd half expected him to break into a chorus of "Always Look on the Bright Side of Life" from behind the hotel desk. Staying at Mar Azul felt like visiting the home of an old friend who was ever so happy to see her; exactly what she needed four years ago and a pleasure that hadn't worn off.

"I've given you the room on the west corner at the front. I recall you being rather a sunset junkie." Paul pushed a key card across the desk.

"Yes, and sunrise. I guess I like the sun, period. And those moments when it's coming up or going down are the most magical. Don't you think?"

"Indeed." Paul nodded and smiled as he typed something into the computer.

"Especially here in Baja where sun means warm. At home the sun can shine beautifully on a day that's minus thirty."

Paul shook his head. "I have no idea how you Canadians do it."

"There's no such thing as bad weather, only inappropriate clothing. At least that's what we tell ourselves."

"But do you believe it?" He raised his eyebrows.

"Not really. If we did you wouldn't find so many of us here in the south for the winter. It would be simpler and less expensive to buy another sweater."

Paul chuckled. "Well, you know your way around so make yourself at home." He glanced up at the clock on the wall. "Sunset is in about half an hour if you want to catch the show before coming downstairs for dinner. I'll send Arturo to get the rest of your bags. Your car is unlocked?"

"It is. Thank you, Paul. But tonight it will be the sunset, a bath and then bed. I'm exhausted, and I had dinner up the road with my Baja caravan companions."

"Still travelling down with the RVers, are you? I guess we'll see you in the morning then. Rest well."

An arched doorway led to a hallway that doubled as Paul's gallery, its white stuccoed walls displaying pieces in watercolour, oil, acrylic, and pastel. Each fall the hotel was taken over by a group of artists led by their British instructor, a friend of Paul's, and many of the pieces had been gifted by the visiting artists. At the end of the hallway was a large open porthole that looked out to the Sea of Cortez. Sandra stopped for a moment to take in the magnificent view: shimmering water, azure sky, the pale beige sand of the beach. She turned left and walked past doors with ceramic signs reading *"Picudos"*, *"Dorado"* and *"Cabrilla"* for some of the fish in the area, and smiled as she arrived at the final door, its indigo sign reading *"Pez Vela"*, Spanish for sailfish. She pushed her card into the slot, turned the handle and entered what would be her home for the next two months. Dropping her bags to the floor, she again closed her eyes to inhale the fragrance of the sea as it blew in through the open French doors. *Heaven.*

Two

What in bloody hell were they squabbling about this morning? He rolled over and buried his face in the pillow, its balloons of goose down pushing up around his ears. The jackhammer in his head was relentless and his mouth felt like the Mojave—much like most mornings these past few weeks. A few weeks? Was that all? It seemed his life had been over longer than that.

Mark turned his head and opened one eye toward the bedside table. He blinked a few times until the red bars of the LED display formed the numbers 10:10. He'd been in bed for—he scrunched his eyelids, trying to sort the numbers in his head—seven hours. At least, he thought he'd called it a night around half-three, but the wee hours of the morning were a bit foggy. Coffee … that's what the situation called for. The coffee machine should have performed its merciful magic by now.

He spread his fingers and pushed his hands into the mattress, raising his torso … and dropped back to the pillow with a groan. If he were at home he'd simply call for Marcia (or was it Marissa?), to fetch him a cup; in this tropical hellhole he was on his own. He rolled onto his side and swung his legs over the edge of the bed, sitting upright. It was then he realized he was still wearing his chinos from the night before. "Sleeping in our clothes now are we? A new high." He rubbed his face with both hands and pushed his fingers through a nest of graying brown hair.

Outside, the squawking of the gulls hit a new crescendo. "Shut up you blasted birds! Get off my verandah!" Mark picked up a shoe and hurled it at the open window, tearing a corner of the screen from its plastic frame. "Messy, noisy, winged demons!" The seagulls continued, seemingly unperturbed by the sudden appearance of flying footwear. He threw the second shoe, striking the wall next to the window. "Flying vermin!"

Mark leaned forward and pulled a shirt from the stack of clothing on a chair next to the bed. Holding it in front of him, he appraised its level of wrinkled-ness and sniffed each of the armpits. "Good enough for this day." With the buttons still fastened, he pulled the shirt over his head as he stood and shuffled toward the living area. His left arm shot through the sleeve opening just as he walked through the bedroom doorway, slamming his hand into the frame. "Damn!" He yanked the garment the rest of the way on and surveyed his throbbing hand, exploring it with the fingers of the other. No blood, nothing broken. He could still hold a cup of coffee.

There was no familiar aroma of Jamaican Blue drifting from the kitchen and no orange rescue light on the coffee machine. He walked to the counter and smacked the side of the machine, hoping for one small miracle in an otherwise dismal morning. Nothing. His eyes drifted left to the scene in the kitchen. Empty wine bottles stood upright on the counter like the last surviving soldiers of the battle surrounded by casualties: oyster shells, a half-eaten plate of fish and rice, a wine glass stained red, a cell phone, and paper, lots of paper. Reams of type-covered paper were strewn everywhere—on the counter, the floor, the stove top, even in the sink.

He stood amidst the rubble and turned a slow circle. *Right. Best get this ruddy mess cleaned up. But first, must have coffee.* He opened the cupboard and observed the space on the shelf that normally housed a bag of coffee beans. "Damn it!" He slammed the door and stood staring at it, daring it to open and again reveal its dearth of coffee. He squeezed his eyes tight and pressed his thumb and forefinger to the bridge of his nose. The gesture seeming to trigger the first pleasant thought in his day: *Paul would have coffee on.*

About House of the Blue Sea

After suffering a devastating loss, artist Sandra Lyall runs south to Mexico seeking solace from her grief. She finds refuge in a small Baja hotel on the edge of the sea to which she returns each winter to continue the healing of her heart. But this year's stay would be different. When a scruffy Englishman with a posh accent offers to buy the painting she's working on, everything changes, and Sandra finds herself torn between her hard-won serenity and her draw to a compelling but risky alternative.

Comments from Readers:

"Teresa van Bryce's debut novel proved not only to be a gentle journey into matters of the heart, but also whispered deeper themes of work, identity, aging and loss. Even the Mexican landscape, described with such vividness, became a character in its own right—making me wish I was there."

"I found myself completely involved in the story. I realized then that 'Of course! This is like Jane Austen's stories, and Jane Eyre, which are among my most beloved books.'"

"A tale of loss, grief, triumph and resilience interspersed with a regular dose of humour."

"You start to know and care about these people, they become your friends and the retreat your own. I was right there with them in their struggles and release. Read this book…"

www.teresavanbryce.com